Keeping Secrets

Adapted by Beth Beechwood

Based on the series created by Michael Poryes and Rich Correll & Barry O'Brien

Part One is based on the episode, "Miley Get Your Gum," Written by Michael Poryes

Part Two is based on the episode, "It's My Party and I'll Lie If I Want To," Written by Douglas Lieblein

WITHDRAWN

DISNEP PRESS

New York

PART ONE

Chapter One

The crowd was going wild after the Hannah Montana concert. But all Hannah could think about was getting offstage and taking off her wig! Then she could go back to being Miley Stewart. Miley was so glad she hadn't told her friends that Hannah Montana—the pop star they were all crazy for—was really just her in disguise! She enjoyed knowing that her friends liked her for who she was, not because she was famous. Only her dad, her brother, and her

3

best friend, Lilly, knew the truth.

"Clear the way, clear the way! Superstar coming through!" Miley's dad, Robby Stewart, shouted to the crowd as he, Miley, and Lilly hurried toward the limo. They all had to wear disguises in order to protect Miley's secret. Lilly was dressed as her alias Lola Luftnagle, and carrying a little Goth lapdog named Thor. Mr. Stewart was in his "Hannah's manager" disguise.

Miley, still dressed as Hannah Montana, always made sure to show her appreciation to the fans. She turned to the crowd and smiled broadly. "Thank you, everybody!" Her strong voice carried the words like a song. "Love to you all! See you next time!"

Though Lilly knew how popular Hannah was, it always surprised her to be in the thick of it. "This is totally insane!" Then, holding Thor up to the crowd, she yelled,

"Back off, people! Back off—don't make me release Thor!"

"Yeah," Miley said, smiling at her brave defender. "You go get 'em, Thor. Two pounds of pure piddle just lookin' for a target."

Looking down and nodding at the puddle surrounding his feet, Mr. Stewart said, "Actually, I think he just found one."

Lilly was embarrassed. "Oh, man!" she cried as they piled into the limo and closed the door. Only, the window was still half open and they could hear someone shouting, "Hold up! Wait!" It was Oliver Oken, Hannah Montana's number one fan.

"Oh, no," moaned Miley. "It's Oliver. *Again*. He snuck into my dressing room last week. He nearly climbed onstage the week before. Just when I think he can't get any more obsessed, *bam!*, he kicks it up a notch!"

Mr. Stewart was entertained, though.

"Look at those bony little elbows go!" he said as Oliver made his way through the throngs. "That boy cuts through a crowd like a Weedwacker."

Miley was anxious. "Close the window!" she commanded. Lilly responded swiftly and the window almost zipped shut, but not before Oliver could thrust his hand inside and stop it from closing all the way.

"Hannah, please!" Oliver begged. "Kiss my hand and I'll never wash it again."

Miley rolled her eyes. "Looks like he never washed it now." Thinking fast, she took Thor from Lilly and poised him right at Oliver's grimy hand. "Come on, Thor, make yourself useful."

Thor gave Oliver's hand a big lick. Fooled, Oliver was beside himself. "Oh, baby, that was a wet one!"

Even when Miley slapped Oliver's hand

out of the way, he was not discouraged.

"Ooh, I like 'em feisty," Oliver swooned as he pulled his hand away. Lilly was able to close the window at long last, and Mr. Stewart turned to the driver.

"You can head out," he said.

Miley was exasperated. "Man," she sighed. "He's never gonna give up."

Lilly got serious. "You better hope he does. Because if he ever finds out your secret, he'll not only be in love with Hannah Montana, he'll be in love with you!"

Miley looked at her friend incredulously. "What? That's crazy! The only thing that's the same about Hannah Montana and me is—" Miley paused for a moment until she realized the truth. "—me." She gathered herself again. "And 'me' doesn't feel that way about him!"

Her dad, however, quickly reassured her.

"Don't worry, Mile, I know guys, and sooner or later he'll get tired of chasing after someone who doesn't chase back." But they all realized it would probably be later rather than sooner. This was Oliver they were talking about. And everyone knew Oliver never gave up.

Just then Mr. Stewart opened the window only to find Oliver furiously peddling his bike alongside the limo. He clutched a small bouquet of flowers in his hand, and as they began to disintegrate in the wind, he shouted, "Do a dude a favor and don't get on the freeway!" But the limo sped up, and Oliver finally started to fall behind, throwing the flowers through the limo window in a last-ditch effort to impress Hannah. "For you, my love!"

Miley shook her head at Thor. "Why did you have to be such a good kisser?"

Chapter Two

The next day at Rico's, a beach hangout, Oliver was holding court with all the guys, telling them the tall tale of "Hannah's" hand kiss. Miley and Lilly had just arrived from the beach, when they overheard Oliver's story. Even Chad the Chomper, who had been busy shooting hoops, stopped long enough to listen.

"It's true," Oliver insisted to the guys. "Hannah actually kissed this hand," he said, pointing to an imaginary spot.

"You gotta be kidding me," said one of the guys he was talking to.

Oliver would not entertain doubters. "A big, slobbery wet one," he said enthusiastically. "Look, it's still shiny."

Lilly couldn't resist. She whispered to Miley, "Yeah, and now every time Oliver calls my house, my dog goes, 'Is it for me, is it for me?'" The girls giggled at their inside joke.

"Chad, dude, close up shop when you chew," Oliver demanded. Chad was chomping on gum a little too dramatically for Oliver's liking. "You're getting spit on the Hannah hand!" Chad wasn't about to listen to Oliver, though. Instead, he shoved another piece of gum into his mouth and chewed even louder. Oliver moved his hand away to protect his precious doggy kiss.

Lilly had had enough. "Mile, let's go. You're cutting into my tan time."

But Miley was distracted. "Look at him, he's never gonna quit. What happens if he does find out? I really care about Oliver. It'd totally weird out our friendship."

Lilly became a little suspicious of her friend, suddenly. "Unless deep, deep down, maybe, just maybe, you feel the same way . . ." They both glanced over at Oliver, who was busy stroking the side of his face with the part of his hand "Hannah" had kissed. The image shook Miley back into reality. "Yes, and maybe, just maybe . . . that's insane!" They laughed and looked on as Oliver continued with his fantasy story.

"Now that she's left her mark on me, it's time to take our relationship to the next level," Oliver said. "Tonight at her CD signing, I'll stare into her eyes and say, 'You're my love, my life, someday you'll be my . . .'" He paused for a moment and stared at the sky, deep in thought. Then, he started to write on his hand, *"Note to self: think of word that rhymes with 'life.'"* Just then, one of the guys pointed out something pretty crucial to Oliver.

"Dude, isn't that the Hannah hand?"

Oliver screamed, "AHHHHH!" Looking sorrowfully down at his hand, he pined, "Forgive me, my love."

The whole incident reminded Miley of something she had forgotten, too. "The CD signing! If he stares into my eyes, he might totally recognize me."

Lilly didn't buy it and brushed off the possibility. "It's never gonna happen."

Miley was still concerned. "But what if it does?"

Lilly looked at her friend seriously. "Then you'll learn to love him like I did with my brother's hamster. And here's the beauty part: if Oliver dies, you won't have to bury him in your backyard."

Sometimes Miley couldn't believe she even knew Lilly. "When you talk, do you hear it, or is there, like, this big roaring in your ears?"

Meanwhile, Oliver was getting more and more irritated as Chad chewed his gum. Chad, clearly amused by this, moved even closer to Oliver's ear and chomped even louder.

"Step off, Chad!" Oliver yelled.

Chad agreed. "Fine. Toss this for me, would ya?" With that, Chad took the wad of gum from his mouth and slapped it down, right on Oliver's precious Hannah hand.

Oliver couldn't take it. "Get it off," he screamed. "Get it off!"

One of the guys to whom Oliver had been bragging earlier looked on curiously.

"What's the deal with you and gum chewing?" he asked Oliver.

Suddenly Oliver was lost in the blurry past. He was back in his crib. He was a baby and all he could remember was an older woman, his Aunt Harriet, leaning over him, chomping on gum. *Chomp, chomp, chomp.* "Look at you, little Ollie," he recalled her saying while she chomped. "Aunt Harriet wants to eat you up." *Chomp, chomp, chomp.* "You're just so yummy, darling . . . yummy, yummy, yummy."

Oliver cringed as he remembered what happened next. Aunt Harriet's gum had fallen right out of her mouth with the last "yummy"—right out of her mouth and onto a very disgusted little Ollie. Oliver shook himself back to the present at Rico's.

"I hate that woman," he said out loud to no one in particular.

Chapter Three

While Miley and Lilly were at the beach and Oliver was shaking off the babyhood memory that had scarred him, Mr. Stewart was on the couch at home, busy writing songs.

". . . Been sittin' here all mornin', tryin' to write a song—can't remember when it took me this dang long . . . maybe I should just up and fly the coop . . . 'cause everything I'm writin' sounds like—" Thankfully, he was interrupted by Miley's older brother, Jackson.

"I got it, Dad! Prepare to be blown away," Jackson announced dramatically.

Mr. Stewart pretended to be annoyed. "This better be good, Son, I was in the middle of a masterpiece."

Jackson put on the voice of a game show host to get his father in the mood for his big news. "Jackson Stewart, come on down!" he bellowed. "You are the proud new owner of a brand-new used car! Yes, over the last fifteen years, this preowned beauty's been driven by heavy smokers, sloppy eaters, and one Wilma McDermott, whose cat popped out six kittens in the front seat — yes, some stains just don't come out!" Jackson finally finished his performance and looked to his dad for a reaction.

"And you're happy about that?" Mr. Stewart asked. Jackson gave it one more shot in his game show voice. "Yes, I am!"

Then he turned serious. "Dad, it's my own car that I bought with my own money."

"I'm proud of ya, Son. Especially that 'my own money' part," he said with a smile as he patted his son on the back. "Let's go take a look at that puppy."

"Ooh, puppies," Jackson said as they walked outside. "That reminds me, in the backseat—"

Mr. Stewart cut him off. "I don't want to know."

They got to the driveway, where they came upon a red convertible. Jackson continued to make a very big deal out of his very big purchase. "Bup-bup-bup-baaaaa!" he sang out proudly.

"Well, would you look at that," Mr. Stewart nodded as he walked around the car, inspecting it carefully. "Clean, no dents and . . . yep," he said after checking out the front seat, "there's that stain." Just then, Jackson's buddy, Cooper, ran up the driveway to meet them. He looked around, puzzled and excited at the same time.

"Where is it?" Cooper demanded of Jackson.

"Right here," Jackson said.

"This?" Cooper asked with a laugh.

Jackson completely understood his friend's doubt. "I can't believe it's mine either," he said.

"And I can't believe you just bought a girl car!" Cooper blurted out.

"What?"

Cooper took a step toward his friend to explain. "Jackson, only girls drive this thing. It's a chick mobile, a babe bucket, a skirt scooter—you might as well have bought a bra with tires, man."

Jackson wouldn't have it. "You are so

wrong. This is totally a guy's car. When I was driving home, there were guys honking, waving, and . . ."

He slowed down, realizing why he'd gotten so much attention, ". . . giving me kissy faces . . . oh, no." Jackson looked to his dad for solace. "Dad, tell me I didn't just buy a chick car," he pleaded.

Straight-faced, Mr. Stewart replied, "You didn't just buy a chick car."

Jackson didn't believe him. "Now say it like you mean it," he demanded.

Leaning in through the driver's window, Mr. Stewart said, "I'd like to, Son, but—" The car bleated out a too-cute *toot-toot*! Mr. Stewart couldn't resist. "You know how ladies like to have the final word."

Chapter Four

Later that night, after the CD signing, Miley's usual entourage piled into the limo. Once again, they had to fight the crowd. Miley was dressed as Hannah, of course, and Lilly and Mr. Stewart were decked out in their "costumes," too. Even Thor was in his little doggy-Goth getup again.

Mr. Stewart fought to close the door as Miley shouted, "Thanks for coming! Love you! Love you all!" The door slammed shut.

"Okay, driver," Mr. Stewart said. "Let's boogie."

Miley excitedly whipped off her wig. "That was great! Oliver looked right into my eyes and never had a clue."

Lilly nodded. "Kind of like the look he has in Spanish." She laughed. The two girls turned to each other and imitated the slightly confused, but mostly blank, stare Oliver always had in Spanish class. *"No comprendo!"* they yelled in unison.

"I don't know what I was so worried about, anyway," Miley said as she settled in and relaxed.

Mr. Stewart opened the moonroof to let in some fresh air.

"Ahh!" They all screamed as Oliver's head popped into the limo from above. Thinking quickly, Miley grabbed Thor and put him right in front of her face. Immediately, her father put her wig back on, albeit slightly askew.

"Don't be scared!" Oliver announced. "It's me, Oliver Oken!"

Mr. Stewart was not pleased. "Driver, pull over!" he demanded.

"Wow, you're even more beautiful upside down," Oliver said to Miley as he hung from the roof.

"Well, thank you," Lilly replied. Miley gave her friend a look.

"He was talking to me," she said. Then she looked up at Oliver and pleaded, "Look, you're very sweet, but you have to stop doing this because . . ." Miley paused, trying to come up with a reason he should stop. *What would make him stop all this?* She had it. ". . . because I have a boyfriend!"

Oliver was visibly stunned. "A boyfriend?" He looked hurt. "I don't understand. Then why did you kiss me?" he asked.

Miley sighed and picked up Thor. "I

didn't kiss you," she explained. "He did."
Well, if no one else had a thing for Oliver,
Thor certainly did. As soon as Miley held
him up to Oliver, he started licking Oliver's
face furiously.

Oliver was mortified. "Oh, man. Those
are the lips I've been thinking about for the
last twenty-four hours?"

Miley felt bad now. "I'm sorry," she said.
"I was trying not to hurt your feelings, but
I'm just not interested. Okay?" She was
trying to be as careful as possible with her
fragile friend.

"Okay," Oliver moped. "I get it."

Mr. Stewart stepped in now. "That's
good, son. Now get off this roof before you
dent it. This is a rental."

"Fine," Oliver replied. "I won't bother
you anymore."

Lilly tried to help ease his pain. "If it

helps, the dog hasn't stopped talking about you," she said hopefully.

Oliver was clearly upset. "You must think I'm pathetic," he said to Miley.

"No," she said gently. "I think you're sweet. And maybe, if I didn't have a boyfriend . . ."

"I'd have a chance with you!" Oliver interrupted her with his old gusto.

Miley tried not to panic. "I never said that," she said anxiously.

"But you implied it!" Oliver wasn't going to let her off the hook now. "And that's enough! I'll wait for you forever!"

"I never said that!" Miley cried. But it was no use. As Oliver pulled his head out of the moonroof, she could hear him shouting. . . .

"Forever! Do you hear me, Hannah Montana?! Forever!" His voice finally faded away.

Lilly was relieved. "Man, that was close," she said to Miley. "He almost caught you tonight."

"Ya think?" she said to Lilly with extreme sarcasm in her voice. "Why do I have to be so irresistible?"

Mr. Stewart piped up with a solution he had been pondering. "You know what that boy needs?" he asked the group rhetorically. "A *real* girlfriend."

Miley started to dismiss her father's idea. "Dad, that is . . ." Then, as she spoke, she realized he might be right. "That is the smartest thing you've ever said!" she shouted gleefully.

Mr. Stewart nodded. "Yeah, well, every now and again even a blind pig snorts up a truffle."

Lilly raised her eyebrows. "And that's the weirdest."

Chapter Five

The next morning at school, a kid struggling to open his locker called out to Oliver. "Yo, Locker Man!"

"I'm on it," Oliver said confidently. And without even breaking his stride, he pounded on the corner of the locker. Just like that, the sticky door flew open. Oliver could fix a stuck locker better than anyone.

"I owe you," the kid said gratefully.

"I'll be back to collect," Oliver replied

over his shoulder as he headed toward his next gig.

"Locker Man," a girl in distress called to him. This would be easy. Oliver spun himself around and elbowed the center of the girl's locker, which popped right open. "You're amazing, Oliver," she cooed.

"I've been told that," Oliver winked. Then he noticed Chad passing by. "Having trouble with your locker, Chad?" he asked smugly.

"Yeah," Chad grunted.

"Well, Locker Man is on the job," Oliver said. "B-But not for you, *sucka*." Just then, Miley approached Oliver. She was about to put her dad's plan into action.

"Oliver, see that girl, Pamela, over there?" she asked, pointing to a cute girl across the hall. "She thinks you're cute." Miley prayed he'd take the bait.

"Can't say that I disagree," Oliver shrugged. "Too bad I'm already cruisin' down the Hannah Highway."

Miley looked down the hallway and spied another girl for Oliver. "What about Kyla Goodwin? She's so desperate, she'll go out with anybody," Miley insisted.

Oliver considered this option. "Usually my type of woman, but I'm taken," he said.

Miley was getting desperate, until she spotted Lilly approaching them. She pulled her friend over to them. "Hey, how about Lilly?! You guys would be perfect together."

Lilly was not happy with Miley at this moment. "Excuse me?" she asked.

Miley forged ahead with her plan, despite the likelihood that Lilly might kill her later. "You're both stubborn," she pointed out.

In unison, Oliver and Lilly said, "I am not!"

"You always agree with each other," Miley said.

"No, we don't," the two of them answered.

"Yes," Miley nodded. "I am definitely seeing a couple here."

Oliver and Lilly turned to each other, overlapping their words, "You're not? Because I'm not . . . Phew."

Miley liked where this was going. She changed her plan, midcourse. "And that's smart," she said, referring to the fact that the two friends weren't actually interested in each other that way. "Because what if one friend loved another but didn't get loved back?" she asked earnestly. "Then things would get all weird, and the friends couldn't be friends anymore." She paused. "And nothing is more important than our friendship, Oliver," Miley said slowly, hoping he would get it.

But Oliver didn't get it at all. "Oh, man!" he shouted. "You love me!"

"No!" Miley said quickly. "I mean, I do love you, but like a brother, or . . . a pet fish." She was fumbling for the right words. "I mean, I'd cry if I had to flush you down the toilet, but I don't want to kiss you." She prayed she was making herself clear.

"That's a relief," Oliver replied. "Because you're my buddy, and I think Hannah and you could wind up being close friends," he said seriously.

Lilly muttered, "Closer than you think."

"Great! Once Hannah and I are together, we'll have you out to the island." Oliver was getting more and more worked up as he talked. "We're going to get an island!" Miley banged her head against a locker in frustration. Then, she and Lilly watched as

Oliver practically skipped away from them toward his locker.

With just a few taps, his locker promptly popped open. He was Locker Man, after all. Inside was a picture of Hannah. "Soon, my love, we'll be together," he swooned. Only this moment between Oliver and his picture of Hannah didn't last long. Chad the Chomper just couldn't leave it alone. He stretched the wad of gum until it reached Oliver's precious Hannah, sticking it right on her. Then, he pulled the rest of the wad from his mouth and let it dangle from poor Hannah's likeness.

"This isn't over, pal!" Oliver shouted as Chad walked off. Then, turning to the picture, he said, "Good-bye, Hannah 102," and he pulled the picture off his locker. "Hello, Hannah 103!" he said, staring at the exact same picture of Hannah.

Lilly and Miley witnessed this whole incident. Now, Miley watched as Lilly got a certain mischievous look in her eye. "I know that look," Miley said. "Either you have a great idea or you really gotta go."

"Oliver is about to totally get turned off to Hannah Montana," she said, and then paused. "And I really gotta go!"

Chapter Six

Jackson Stewart couldn't care less about what was going on with Miley, Lilly, and Oliver. He had much bigger things to worry about. He and his dad had just pulled into the driveway in his chick mobile. "I can't believe he wouldn't take the car back," Jackson said to his dad. "I thought I made a very convincing argument."

Mr Stewart gave his son a look. "Technically, getting on your hands and knees and begging for a do-over is not an argument," he explained as they both got out of the car.

"Hey there, neighbor," a voice called out to them.

"Oh, man, it's Mr. Dontzig," Jackson said. "And he's in a robe again." Mr. Dontzig was the Stewarts' neighbor, and he was known for being underdressed and overinvolved in neighborhood concerns.

"Count your blessings," Mr. Stewart said. "At least this time it's the long one." Mr. Dontzig approached them on the driveway, revealing his whole outfit: the long robe over a baggy swimsuit, and a pair of flip-flops on his feet.

"So, Stewart family," he started. "What would another leaf from your tree be doing in my hot tub?" he accused, holding up the guilty leaf.

"Oh, I don't know," Mr. Stewart smirked. "Maybe it wanted to party."

Mr. Dontzig was not amused. "Well, something needs to be done about this."

Mr. Stewart stared at his neighbor's belly and retorted, "And something needs to be done about *that*. I'm suggesting either some sit-ups or a bigger robe."

Jackson pointed to his dad enthusiastically. "Zing!" he shouted.

Mr. Dontzig turned to Jackson's car. "Nice ride, Jackson," he said. "My wife used to have a car like this. Traded it in. She thought it was too girly." He paused then and said, "Get your leaves out of my pool!" He started to leave, but Mr. Stewart wouldn't let the gruff neighbor have the last word.

"I'll have you know, we Stewart men don't define ourselves by the kind of cars we drive," he said proudly as Mr. Dontzig walked off. But to Jackson, his father muttered, "That's it, this dolly wagon's going back to where it came from." And with that, he hopped into the driver's seat.

"But the salesman already said no," Jackson explained.

"To you," Mr. Stewart said. "Not to me. Face it, Son, I'm a little bit more intimidating." He started to back out of the driveway but accidentally hit the horn. *Toot-toot!* "Lord!" he cried. "If I have to choose between that and an accident, I'm taking the accident."

Chapter Seven

Later that day, Lilly and Miley were about to put Lilly's plan into action. Lilly had called Oliver and told him to meet her at a remote part of the beach. She also shared some startling news about Hannah Montana. Now, Lilly was hiding behind a big rock, waiting for Oliver to arrive.

Oliver came running up to her. Breathlessly, he said, "I came as fast as I could! Is she still here?"

Lilly pointed to Miley, who was in

Hannah mode. "Right over there."

"I can't believe you saw Hannah Montana break up with her boyfriend right here on our beach, at the exact moment I was getting home from the orthodontist."

"I know," Lilly said in her best faux-dramatic voice. "Knock, knock, who's there? Fate."

"Fate who?" Oliver never understood Lilly's sense of humor.

"Just go!" Lilly commanded.

Oliver gathered himself. He had to get psyched up for his moment. "Okay," he said breathing deeply. "This is it. . . ."

"Good luck, Oliver," Lilly bubbled. "But remember, if it doesn't work, you're still 'Smokin' Oken.'"

"Thanks," Oliver answered. "But it's gonna work out."

"Absolutely!" Lilly assured him. "But if it

doesn't . . . Smokin' Oken. 'Nuff said."
Lilly walked away then, and Oliver headed
bravely toward his destiny.

He approached Hannah, who was sitting
with her back to him. "Hi, it's me, Oliver,"
he said. "I heard about your breakup and
I'm here for you. If you need a hug, my
arms are open." This was all very nice of
course, sweet, even. If only he had actually
said it to Hannah! The "girl" who had had
her back to him turned around to reveal
that she wasn't Hannah Montana at all.
She wasn't even a girl. She was a he.

"Get away from me, you pasty-faced little freak!" the guy shouted.

Oliver retreated. "I can do that," he said
as he backed away carefully. Then, he spotted another blond girl with her back to him.
This time, he was more careful. "Hannah?"
he asked.

Miley, as Hannah—giant sunglasses, blond wig, and all—was chomping on a giant wad of chewing gum. When she turned to Oliver, her cheeks were positively swollen and she was drooling. "Hey, the kid from the moonroof. Look at you, all upside right," she slurped.

Oliver was stunned. Put off, even. "Whoa," he said as she shoved yet another piece of gum into her very crowded mouth.

"Where are my manners?" Hannah exclaimed. "Sit down, sweetie, join the party." Hannah grabbed Oliver and put him in her chair. "You want some gum? Here." She handed him a pack of bubble gum. "Load yourself up."

"I didn't know you liked gum," Oliver stammered. "I've surfed all of your Web sites, and none of them said you were a chewer." He didn't quite know how to process this new "wad" of information.

"Oh," Hannah said, chomping right in Oliver's face, "I love to chew. I chew all the time. Like a train—chew, chew, chew." As she chewed, chewed, chewed in his face, Oliver suddenly couldn't get the image of Aunt Harriet out of his head. Hannah continued, "I chew in the morning, the afternoon, the evening; I love it. If it can be chewed, it's in my mouth."

Oliver stood up. He couldn't believe it, but he wanted to put some distance between himself and Hannah. "Good to know," he said as he backed away. "You might want to think about updating your Web sites."

"Why?" Hannah asked in an overly earnest way. "Does it bother you? It really turns off some people. They can't even be around me. They love me, but I disgust them," she explained.

"Well," Oliver announced. "I'm not like that."

Now Miley was getting worried. This *had* to work. "You're not? Because it's okay if you are." She hoped, hoped, hoped that he was like that.

"No," Oliver said decisively. "Relationships are about sacrifice. I accept you . . . just the way you are."

Miley started to freak out. Was it possible this wasn't working? She had to up the ante. "Good to know," she said, shoveling another piece of gum into her already stuffed mouth. "Move over, boys. New chew comin' through." She started to chew like a cow, even harder and more disgustingly than she even thought she could.

Oliver was so horrified he couldn't look away. "Your . . . mouth," he started to say. "It's . . . it's . . ."

"Turning black?" Hannah asked brightly. "It's licorice. My favorite. Just don't make me laugh. It comes out my nose. Wanna see?"

"No!" Oliver screamed.

"Too late!" Hannah yelled. "She's about to blow!" Oliver thought fast and grabbed her nose. He had to keep the black stuff in. It would be too much for him to bear. He loved Hannah, but this was just . . . too much. "Am I grossing you out?" Miley asked. "Because I totally understand if you hate me now and want to transfer your obsession to Mandy Moore. You know, she's blond again."

Oliver let go of Hannah's nose and braced himself for the worst. "No," he said. "My love is bigger than my disgust and your . . . black . . . drippage."

Miley was thoroughly frustrated. This

guy wouldn't give up. She had to pull out all the stops. "Speaking of black drippage, check this out!" She started to blow a bubble, a big, big bubble.

Oliver watched in horror. "Sacrifice, sacrifice, sacrifice," he chanted to himself. Hannah's bubble started to get out of control. Oliver looked on as it grew and grew, until it could grow no more. Then, it burst right in Oliver's face!

"How do you like me now?" Hannah shouted in complete exasperation.

"I . . . I . . . still love you!" Oliver declared.

Like the big black bubble, Hannah finally exploded. "What does it take with you? What more do I have to do? You and Hannah are never going to be together," she ranted.

"Why not?" Oliver asked.

"Because . . ." Scanning the beach quickly

to make sure no one was around, she pulled off her wig and glasses. "I'm Hannah Montana. Me. Miley."

Oliver went stiff, then started to hyperventilate. He promptly passed out.

Miley stared down at him. "Okay, that went well."

Chapter Eight

When Oliver came to, he had a lot of questions for his friend. He paced back and forth in front of her as she sat on the beach, bracing herself for his rampage. "So, you were Hannah Montana in the limo, when I was upside down?" he asked.

"Yes," Miley answered.

"And backstage when I was hanging out the window?"

"Yup."

"And when I hid in the bass drum and

rode on your tour bus all the way to Phoenix?"

"You did what?" Miley's voice went up an octave in disbelief.

"Nothing." Oliver dismissed her and then stopped pacing. "How could you not tell me?"

"I'm sorry, but you were just so in love with Hannah, and I was afraid you might be . . ."

"In love with you? Do you think I am?"

"You tell me. I mean, have you ever pictured yourself buying an island with me, Miley, your friend, the dork?"

"You're not a dork."

"Oh, come on. What about the time I tripped in biology lab and spilled frog juice all over you?"

"Oh, right, Mom made me take off my pants in the school parking lot."

"Or when we were at Andrew's birthday party and you knocked me into the pool in your one-man stampede for the cake?" Miley reminded him.

"That's not fair," Oliver whined. "It was an ice-cream log cake! And you know I have to get an end cut!"

"Okay," Miley said, "what about the time we had to do that scene from *Romeo and Juliet*, and you couldn't even kiss me without cringing?" she asked.

"Well, those onion rings you ate before class didn't help," Oliver pointed out in his defense.

"Come on, Oliver." Miley was serious now. "Was it the onion rings or was it me?"

Oliver looked at her intently. "I guess it was a little of both," he admitted.

"Oliver, face it," Miley said to her friend. "The girl you thought you loved is standing right here, and the truth is, you don't love her."

She had a really good point. Oliver had to take that in for a moment. "Wow," he said. "I think you're right. That's two years of my life I'll never get back."

Miley nodded. "Sorry about that," she said. "So . . . what do you think? Are we gonna be okay?"

"Yeah. We're okay." They looked at each other for a minute, then hugged.

"So, you feel anything?" Miley asked as they hugged.

"Nope," Oliver said, still hugging her. "In fact, it's a little awkward." They broke apart and then regrouped.

"Come on, let's go grab a hot dog," Miley suggested.

"Sure, and you can have all the onions you want," Oliver joked.

As they walked off, Oliver remembered something.

"Hannah," he said. "So, Mandy Moore," he mused. "You don't happen to have her number, do you?"

Miley pretended to be insulted that he had gotten over her already. "Boy, you bounce back fast," she teased. The two walked happily toward Rico's, and all was well again.

Meanwhile, Jackson was still sweating his bad-car day. He and Cooper were hanging out in the driveway at the Stewarts' house, waiting for Mr. Stewart to return with hopefully good news. Cooper was busy shooting hoops as Jackson paced and looked at his watch every other second.

"Where is my dad?" he asked, frustrated. "It's been hours. He couldn't sell it. That's what it is. He couldn't sell it and now he can't face me."

Cooper tried to look on the bright side. "You don't know that. Maybe something good happened—maybe he parked it somewhere and a bunch of cheerleaders stole it," he joked.

"Yeah, like I have that kind of luck," Jackson said. Then, just as Jackson had feared, his dad drove up in the same girly car he had left in. "Oh, here he comes. Still driving it. I knew it. Failure! You're a failure as a father!" he shouted.

"Get a grip, Son," Mr. Stewart said, trying to calm down his hysterical child. "I couldn't get rid of the car, but I did do a little somethin' to beef it up a bit." He honked the horn then, and out came a blast that an eighteen-wheeler might make. It was the horn of a big rig.

"Dad," Jackson said, "changing the horn's not gonna make it a guy car."

"I know," Mr. Stewart admitted, "but this might." Jackson and Cooper watched as Jackson's father pushed a button and the trunk popped open. Suddenly, lights started flashing and the stereo started booming. Mr. Stewart had tricked out Jackson's ride, and it was cool.

"Dang, this is tight," Cooper admitted.

Mr. Stewart was proud of himself. As he got out of the car, he said to Jackson, "Son, I primped your ride."

"Oh, yes, he did!" Cooper yelled.

"Thank you, Dad, thank you!" Jackson jumped up, hugged, and hung on to his father.

"Okay, Son, you can let go," Mr. Stewart said, extricating himself a little from the hug. Nevertheless, Jackson clung to him tightly, still refusing to let go. "That was cute when you were five," he said. "Now it just throws my back out."

Jackson finally let go, giving his dad a break. But Cooper didn't let Mr. Stewart rest very long.

"My turn!" he shouted as he jumped on Mr. Stewart just like Jackson had.

"Yep, there it goes!" Mr. Stewart said, reaching for his lower back. Oh, well, at least his children's crises were averted for now. That was all he could ask for!

PART TWO

Chapter One

It was a concert night and Miley, dressed as Hannah, was in the middle of a quick, last-minute warm-up with Kay, her vocal coach.

"I'm a lucky girl, whose dreams came true," Hannah sang. "But underneath it all, I'm just like you." She trailed off. "How's that?" she asked Kay.

"Perfect," Kay replied, smiling.

Then, they heard the stage manager calling to them. "Hannah Montana, you're on in two minutes," he shouted.

"All right," Kay said seriously. "Shake the nerves out." Hannah shook her shoulders loosely. "Good," Kay said. "Get it out. Loosen up the throat."

Kay directed Hannah to do a little vocal exercise, and Hannah complied, "Ah, ah, ah, ah. . . ." Then Hannah took the shaking to a whole new level—an animal level. She started bouncing and shaking, dancing and screeching . . . like a monkey. Then, just as suddenly as she let the animal take her over, she snapped out of it. "Okay," she said in a completely normal voice, "good to go."

Kay laughed. "Remember when I started coaching you, and you were embarrassed to do that?" Kay looked wistful. "I miss those days." She walked off then, leaving Hannah alone. Not long after, two of her "industry" friends walked in.

"Traci, Evan, I'm so glad you guys are here! You having fun?" she asked her guests, who knew her only as Hannah Montana. Traci and Evan had no idea that Hannah had a whole other *normal* life as Miley Stewart, eighth grader!

"Tons of," Traci replied. Traci was the ultrahip daughter of Hannah's record producer. She knew everything and everyone. "Except there's this weird girl in your dressing room who keeps sticking her tongue in the chocolate fountain." Traci made a disgusted face.

"She looked like my dog in a rain puddle," Evan chimed in.

"It was a major party foul," Traci said. "Oh, no," she continued, looking in the direction of a disguised Lilly. "There she is."

There she was, all right. Lilly, dressed as her alias, Lola Luftnagle, walked into the room. As evidence of Traci and Evan's accusations, she had a chocolate ring around her mouth.

"Hannah!" Lilly shouted.

Traci was surprised. "You know her?"

"Look at this," Lilly said, referring to her cell phone. "I was in the bathroom and got a picture of a very famous finger picking a very famous nose! How great is that?"

Hannah stepped toward her friend and gently closed the offending cell phone. "Okaaay," she said sarcastically. "Thanks for sharing. Traci and Evan, this is my friend, uh . . ." She had forgotten Lilly's alias! She looked to Lilly, hoping her friend would stop shoveling strawberries into her mouth long enough to help her out. Thankfully, Lilly caught on.

"Lola Luftnagle," she said, with her mouth full. "Daughter of oil baron

Rudolph Luftnagle, sister of socialites Bunny and Kiki Luftnagle, cousin of . . ." Hannah elbowed Lilly in the ribs, and she stopped herself. "But you can call me Lola," she said to Traci and Evan, inadvertently spitting some strawberry juice in Traci's face. "Whoops!" she exclaimed. "My bad!"

Traci was less than pleased. "Yes, it is."

Hannah intervened before things got even worse. Stepping between Lilly and Traci, she said, "Soooo, you guys gonna hang backstage?"

"Hey," Lilly shouted. "That'd be cool! We could hang together!" she said to Traci and Evan.

Evan tried to get out of hanging with Lola. "But, then . . . who would sit in our seats?"

"Good point," Traci agreed. "And it is

getting a little crowded back here."

"I see what you mean," Lilly said, not understanding that Traci was referring to Lilly herself! "Who let some of these people backstage?"

"Really," Traci and Evan said in unison. "Tell me about it." Then, as they walked off, Traci said in a snotty voice, *"Hasta la pasta."* Traci waited until she was out of Hannah and Lilly's range before saying to Evan, "What a loser."

Lilly really had no idea what was going on. "They seem nice. Maybe I should go with them?" Lilly started to walk toward Traci and Evan. Hannah quickly pulled her back.

"Nooo . . . 'cause you're my good luck charm," she said, wiping Lilly's face with her towel. "My chocolate-covered good luck charm."

"Whoa," Lilly said, seeing how chocolaty the towel was. "That's embarrassing."

"Oh, you can hardly see it," she tried to reassure her friend. And yet, she yelled off to the stage manager, "I'm gonna need another towel!"

"Now," she said to Lilly, "I want you to stay right here where I can see you—and no one else will," she said emphatically. "Just pretend those little feet are nailed to the ground."

From the stage, they heard the announcer cry, "Are you ready, San Diego?" The crowd roared. "Then let's hear it! Hannah Montana!" The crowd roared even louder.

Hannah looked seriously at Lilly. "Just nailed right there. Tap, tap, tap."

"Don't worry, 'Hannah.' 'Lola' will be right here for you," Lilly assured her friend. Hannah headed onto the stage to thunderous applause from her fans and started singing with her signature gusto. Lilly watched her friend, keeping her promise to stay put . . . until . . .

"The bathrooms are over here, Ms. Stefani," she heard someone say as a group of people walked by, all surrounding a certain platinum-blond pop star.

Lilly hesitated at first, but staying put was a lot to ask in this particular situation. "Gwen Stefani!" she yelled, finally running off toward the entourage. "Gwen, babe, wait up. I'll go with you. Why are you running? Gwenny? Gwendela!"

Hannah noticed this from the stage but could do nothing but hope for the best.

Chapter Two

The next day, Miley had a lot on her mind and no one to talk to. There was her dad, asleep on the couch, his mouth hanging wide open and his guitar leaning on a chair nearby. Miley didn't want to bother him, but she really needed some advice. She decided to be subtle, sitting down next to her father and sighing lightly. Nothing, not a twitch. She sighed again, louder. Still nothing. Time to try something a little more direct.

"Wake up!" she shouted.

Robby Stewart jumped, and Miley sighed with relief—her dad was definitely awake now. "Darlin', sometimes I wish you came with a snooze button," he said, shaking off his nap. "Now, what's this all about?"

"Lilly," Miley said dramatically. "I don't know what to say to her. I mean, I don't want to hurt her feelings, but she was so embarrassing backstage." As she spoke, Jackson, Miley's older brother, came down the stairs and grabbed some popcorn.

"How bad was it?" Mr. Stewart asked, referring to Lilly's backstage behavior.

Jackson happily piped up. "Let's just say Lilly made a little unscheduled trip last night to Dork Flats, Iowa. Population: her," he said as he headed for the kitchen.

Mr. Stewart followed his son while he calmed Miley. "Come on, Mile, she's just not used to being backstage. I'm sure next time she—"

Miley interrupted her father and said, "*Won't* follow Gwen Stefani into the bathroom and ask her to sign her protective seat cover?!" Miley's dad and brother started laughing. "It ain't funny," she said to them.

Mr. Stewart put on a serious face. "No, it's not," he said, looking at Jackson, "What's wrong with you, boy?"

Miley was exasperated. "You just don't know what it's like to have someone you love embarrass you all the time." The conversation came to a halt as Miley and her dad watched Jackson pour a heaping spoonful of powdered chocolate into his mouth, then swig a big gulp of milk and shake his head to mix them up while jumping up and down for good measure. Then, at last, he swallowed his "chocolate milk."

"Oh, I think I do," Mr. Stewart said to Miley.

The phone rang and Jackson answered it, his mouth still thick with his concoction. "Hello?" He hung up the phone, then said to Miley and Mr. Stewart, "Lilly landing in three . . . two . . . one."

As usual, Miley opened the front door just as Lilly sailed in on her skateboard. "That concert last night was so much fun. I had so much fun. Did you have so much fun?" Lilly asked as she skidded to a halt in the kitchen.

Jackson put on his best girl voice and started to mock his sister. "I had fun! Did you see the dreamy boy in the third row? Woo!"

"We do not sound like that!" Miley insisted to her brother. "And he was in the second row."

As Jackson and Miley argued, Lilly reenacted the very same chocolate-milk–making method Jackson had displayed just moments before. Mr. Stewart walked over and took the milk away from Lilly after she swigged it. "Come on, people, I make pancakes with that milk!" he complained.

At that moment, the distinctive tone of Hannah Montana's cell phone filled the room.

"Yes!" Lilly exclaimed. "The Hannah line—it's always somebody so cool! Let me answer it this time!" she begged.

"No, no, I'll get it," Miley said as she flipped her phone. "Yo-la!" Miley said as she put the phone to her ear. Lilly wouldn't let up. She moved close to the phone and put her ear to the other side of it. Even as Miley moved away from her friend, Lilly followed.

It was Traci on the line. "Hey, superstar, it's Trace."

"What's going on?" Miley asked.

"We're throwing a little birthday party for Kelly tonight—"

"Kelly?" Lilly asked. "Kelly Clarkson?" Again, Miley tried to move away from Lilly, to no avail.

Traci continued, "And if you don't come, I'll get all pouty."

"Ahhh!" Lilly shouted gleefully. "This is so cool. We're going to Kel-*lay*'s par-*tay*!" She started to dance in celebration.

Miley covered the mouthpiece and looked at her jig-dancing friend. "What are you doing?" she asked Lilly.

"I'm doing my 'I'm going to Kel-*lay*'s par-*tay*' dance," Lilly replied.

Still covering the phone, Miley said, "And I love it. It's just that . . . I'm not sure I can bring anybody."

"Well, ask her," Lilly insisted.

"Ask her. Yes. I should do that."

"Now!" Lilly demanded.

"Now. Yes. I should do that . . . now."

Lilly jammed her head next to Miley's as Miley asked Traci questions. "So, Trace . . . I can't bring anybody, right?" She prayed for a no, even as Lilly was praying just as hard for a yes.

"Sure, Kelly said you can bring anybody you want," Traci said, confirming Miley's fear.

Lilly, on the other hand, was ecstatic. "Yes!" she yelled right into the phone. "Trace, it's Lola! I'll see you there!"

Sitting in the recording studio on her cell phone, Traci said back to Lola, "Loving it." Then, she too covered the phone and said to herself, "Hating her."

"This is so cool. I can't believe I'm actually going to a big Hollywood party!" Lilly said. "Excuse me." Lilly walked out onto the deck, closed the door behind her, and they all watched as she did her happy dance outside.

Traci, however, was not doing a happy dance. "Hannah, I have a micro problem," she said.

"I know, I know, but Lilly—Lola is a really great person once you get to know her." Miley was trying to plead her friend's case.

"Yeah, see, the getting-to-know-her part? That's the problem," Traci replied. Miley braced herself for what she knew was coming. "I mean, she's just so uncool, it's totally embarrassing."

"Yeah, but—" Miley wanted to go to bat for Lilly, but Traci cut her off.

"I knew you'd understand. *Ciao*." Then the line went dead.

Miley didn't know what to do. She headed for the kitchen where Mr. Stewart and Jackson were eating cake—her dad with a fork, her brother with his hands.

"Lilly's not invited, is she?" Mr. Stewart asked.

Miley put her head on her dad's shoulder. "What am I gonna do? Look"—she directed them to Lilly, who was still dancing on the deck. "And that's her before the party. I just wish there was a magic spell that could stop people from acting like . . . geeksicles!"

As Mr. Stewart watched his son try to catapult a marshmallow into his mouth with a spoon, he agreed. "Me, too."

Chapter Three

Later that day, Jackson was working the counter at Rico's, serving Miley's friend Oliver and his coworker and friend Rico some lunch, when a beautiful girl walked into the restaurant. Though the girl smiled at the group, Oliver "Mr. Confidence" Oken stepped right up. "Whoa, older woman, checking me out," he said.

"In your dreams, Oken," Jackson sneered.

Oliver had to concede that point. "Normally, yes, but—"

"She's only lookin' at you," Jackson interrupted, "'cause you're sitting next to me."

"*Playas*, please," Rico said, stepping in. "I'm the man she wants. I'm cute, I'm rich—"

"And you fit in her purse." Jackson couldn't resist. His friend Rico was tiny! "*Muy macho*!"

"Watch and learn, boys," Oliver said, confident that he was in the running for the girl's attention. "But don't applaud; it

"She's only lookin' at you," Jackson interrupted, "'cause you're sitting next to me."

"Oh, I don't have to pretend," she answered, much to Oliver's surprise. "You're cute."

"Really?"

The girl took Oliver's face in her hands then and said in a high-pitched baby voice, "Yes you are. You're the cutest little boy. Look at that face," she squealed as she pinched his cheeks. "And those chubby, chubby cheeks!"

Oliver pulled away, mortified. "Okay, not helping!"

"I'm sorry," she said, still using that sugary voice. "Let me make it all better. Do you want some candy?"

Would the embarrassment never end? "No, I don't want any can—" He paused, intrigued. "What kind is it?" He peeked in her bag and took out a candy bar. Satisfied with himself, Oliver marched back to his buddies at the counter. Jackson and Rico were cracking up.

"Yuck it up, boys," Oliver said, "I got

nougat on the first date." Then he walked away, content to eat his free candy bar.

It was Rico's turn now. He turned to Jackson after Oliver left. "Well, now it's time for a real man. It's 'Rico time.'" True to form, he then licked his fingers, and used them to smooth his eyebrows.

"Yeah," Jackson replied. "It's Rico's bedtime," he said as he hopped over the counter to step ahead of his rival. He looked back at Rico on his way to the older woman. "Get ready to cry yourself to sleep."

Jackson, like Oliver, walked confidently up to the girl and said, "Hi, please pretend to like me, my boss's kid is watching."

"But I do like you," she said.

Thinking she was simply helping a guy out, Jackson said, "That's perfect, just a little more—" He paused, noticing that she seemed to be serious. "Oh."

"I'm Nina," she said.

Jackson happily shook her hand. "Jackson," he said. He couldn't believe this was happening. This girl was gorgeous. Way out of his league. Even he had to admit that.

"Look, I don't mean to be pushy—" Nina continued.

"No, please, push," Jackson insisted. "I like pushy. Pushy is good."

"I'm a student at the Malibu School of Beauty, and I was wondering if I could borrow your head?" Nina asked.

"What?"

"It's just that your hair is so fantastic, and I really need someone to practice on, and I'd give just anything to get my hands on it," she gushed.

"Well, it's your lucky day, anything is exactly my price." Jackson didn't care what she wanted to do with his hair. Any time spent with Nina would be just fine with him. He led her to the counter. "Have a seat," he said.

As he crossed over to his side of the counter he grinned at Rico. "How do I do it?" he asked his friend smugly.

Nina and Rico looked at each other knowingly, as if they knew something Jackson didn't. "You got me," Rico said quietly, laughing a silly, evil laugh. "Or, I got you."

Back at the Stewart household later that day, Jackson started to understand what Rico's evil laugh had been about. Sitting in the middle of his kitchen in a barber's chair, draped with a smock, Jackson stared at himself in a hand mirror.

"Wow. That's . . . interesting," he

stammered. He had orange hair—bright orange hair. What else was there to say?

"I'm so sorry. My parents were right. I don't have what it takes to be a beautician." Nina was practically in tears.

"Of course you do," Jackson reassured her. He couldn't get too mad. She was too pretty. "Don't worry, we can fix this. We can fix this, right?"

"Yeah, let me just go home and practice on my dog one more time. I'll see you tomorrow," she said hurriedly as she got ready to leave.

"Tomorrow?! But what about—"

"You're so sweet and understanding," Nina swooned. She leaned down and kissed him on the forehead, which truly made everything much better for Jackson.

"No worries, I have hats," he said.

Just as Nina ran out, Mr. Stewart walked

in. He spotted Jackson's new look right away. "Don't start," Jackson said to his father.

"It's okay, Son. Heck, I've done my share of crazy things to get in good with a girl." He looked harder at his son's head. "Nothing as . . . orange as that. See, in my day we had a little thing called pride."

"In your day, you had a little thing called a mullet," Jackson retorted.

"And it was a thing of beauty. Business in the front, party in the back." Mr. Stewart got lost in the memory for a moment, until he realized his son wasn't laughing. He walked over to Jackson and put his arms around him. "Listen, from what I can tell, she's a real nice girl. Just keep your eye on the prize."

Mr. Stewart left then, leaving Jackson there by himself. Only, he wasn't really alone. Peeking in the window was Rico, who was very proud of himself. If Jackson had turned around just then, he would have seen Rico laughing that evil laugh and wringing his evil hands in celebration. Instead, Jackson just felt an eerie chill as a flash of lightning lit up Rico's creepy face lurking at the window.

Chapter Four

Later that day, Jackson was hanging out in the kitchen, pondering his new carrot top, when Miley came in. She was dressed as Hannah, in preparation for the big party.

"Hey, shouldn't you be at that party?" Jackson asked his sister.

"I'm going. I just have to tell Lilly the truth first. I know it's gonna be hard, but it's the right thing to do." Miley was dreading telling her friend the news.

Suddenly, Jackson let out a big, dramatic, "No! No! It hurts so baaaaad!"

"What are you doing?" Miley asked.

"An imitation of Lilly in about two minutes," Jackson replied, as if he knew everything. "Now if you want to avoid that, here's a little tip from your big brother: lie like a rug."

"Yeah, I'm really gonna take advice from a guy who looks like a traffic cone." Miley couldn't resist mocking her know-it-all brother. Besides, he had orange hair. He *did* look like a traffic cone.

But Jackson was quick with a comeback, as always. "Traffic cones save lives," he said on his way out. Miley shook her head at her brother and went to the front door to greet Lilly. Ah, Lilly. There she was when Miley opened the door. Dressed as Lola, she danced, in a one-girl conga line into the living room.

"Par-*tay*, par-*tay*, par-*tay*!" she sang. "Par-*tay*, par-*tay*, par-*tay*! Everybody now! Par-*tay*, par-*tay*, par—" Lilly paused, finally noticing that Miley was not joining in with the enthusiasm she expected. In fact, Miley was not joining in at all. "Hey, what's wrong?"

Miley took a deep breath and said, "Lilly, we have to talk."

Lilly shrugged this off. "Well, let's talk on the way to the par-*tay*," she suggested.

"No, Lilly, we have to talk now," Miley said firmly. She took her friend's arm and urged her over toward the couch.

Now, Lilly was visibly concerned. "Why? What's the matter?" she asked as they sat down.

"Okay, we've always promised to be honest with each other, right?" Miley asked, hoping this conversation was going to go well.

"Yeah," Lilly said.

"No matter how hard that might be," Miley continued.

Lilly was very worried now. "Are you trying to tell me this shirt doesn't go with these pants?" she asked with alarm in her voice.

Miley paused to think about this. "Yes," she said. The pants didn't go at all. "But also . . . okay, I'm just going to say it. The truth is . . ." She saw the concern in Lilly's face and couldn't go through with it. "The party's canceled," she said instead.

Lilly was crushed, of course, but not nearly as crushed as she would have been had Miley actually told her the truth. Miley just couldn't do that to her friend. However, she couldn't miss the party, either, so after Lilly went home to study, Miley headed to the party . . . alone.

Miley waited outside for her dad to pick her up from the club where the party was being held. She had gone in and just didn't feel right. Her guilt was eating her up with every celebrity she spotted. Poor Lilly. Miley was almost free and clear, when Traci spotted her.

"Hannah, I've been looking all over for you. What are you doing out here?" she asked.

"I'm waiting for my dad to pick me up," she answered, trying to sound casual.

"But Kelly's not even here yet," Traci pleaded.

"I know, but I guess I'm just not feeling in a party mood tonight," she said.

"Okay, love you, but you're downin' my

vibe. T-T-Y-L." And she was off, headed back into the club. It was just like Traci not to care why "Hannah" wasn't in a party mood. Just then, Miley's cell phone rang, and before she thought to check the caller ID, she picked up.

"Hello?"

"So, whatcha doing?" It was Lilly. Of course it was Lilly.

"Lilly?! Um . . ." Miley had to think fast. Why did she pick up? "I'm not doing anything. Nothing. Just . . . studying. No party. Just me. Party of one." Could it be any worse than this? And of course, the door to the club opened at that very moment, and there was a loud hiss of music and crowd noise.

"What's that?" Lilly asked.

"Oh. That's . . ." She closed the door herself. "That's just Jackson playing his stereo too loud." She pretended to shout to Jackson. "Jackson, turn it down! I'm studying, fool!" Then, when she saw how the bouncer outside the door was looking at her, she whispered to him, "Sorry, not you. Nice nose ring."

Lilly didn't seem fazed. "So, you want to go to the mall tomorrow?" she asked cheerfully.

"Sure, sounds like fun," Miley answered, relieved that Lilly wasn't more suspicious. But, just as relief set in, some paparazzi approached and yelled, "Hannah Montana, say 'cheese'!" Oh, that's just *perfect*, Miley thought.

"Who's that?" Lilly asked.

"My dad . . ." Miley said, hoping Lilly would buy this one, too. Then, pretending to yell back to her dad, "No, Dad, I don't want extra cheese!" But, the paparazzi wouldn't let up. She noticed they were taking her picture. "I gotta hang up," she said to Lilly, "before he goes all deep-dish on me."

Miley had to nip this one in the bud. Her lie would be exposed if someone printed those pictures and Lilly saw them, which she definitely would, since Lilly read every celebrity magazine and newspaper there was. She approached the photographer. "Hi," she said sweetly. "I have a friend who can't know that I'm here, so I was wondering if y'all could be a good guy and not print that picture."

"Sure, sweetheart, no problem," one photographer said, as if he was going to comply. "Oh, wait, I'm not a good guy." The photographer thought his little joke was pretty funny. He laughed and snapped yet another picture of her.

He turned to walk away, but Miley was fed up. "Well, in that case, I'm not a good girl." With that, she jumped on his back and tried to grab the camera out of his hands. Well, this struggle attracted quite a bit of attention—just the kind of attention Miley was trying to avoid! Miley looked up to see a hail of flashbulbs explode in her face. And to make matters worse, there was a video crew capturing the whole thing. This was not going to be good.

Chapter Five

It was even worse than Miley thought. Her picture was plastered across the front page of the L.A. *Herald*'s entertainment section. HANNAH'S WILD RIDE was the headline, and the picture wasn't pretty. Miley had a lot of work to do. There was no way she could let Lilly see the paper. It was irrational, but she set out to gather every copy of the *Herald* she could find, so that Lilly wouldn't spot the story.

Meanwhile, at the Stewart home, Jackson was defending yet another disaster, courtesy of the world's worst beauty school student. Now, Jackson was sporting a blue Mohawk! When Mr. Stewart walked in from his run, Jackson was quick to pre-empt his father's jokes. "She was just trying to even out the sides!" he yelled defensively. "It could have happened to anybody."

"I'm not going to say a thing," Mr. Stewart replied.

"Thank you." Jackson was grateful that his dad was willing to let this one go.

"I'm going to sing a thing," Mr. Stewart said, and then he started singing. "I once knew a girl named Nina, and was she a find. So I gave my sweetie my golden locks. Now I look like a bluebird's behind." Then he started to really belt it out. "Bluebird's behind, bluebird's behind . . ."

Jackson didn't appreciate this one bit. "Whatever happened to using your own misery to write a song?" he asked.

"I'm sorry, Son, I only make fun 'cause I went through it myself. Every man has. At least you can take some comfort in the fact that you got yourself a date with a pretty girl," Mr. Stewart offered.

"Well, not yet," Jackson admitted.

"Ouch," Mr. Stewart said.

Miley entered just in time to save Jackson from more mocking. She had an armful of newspapers. "Okay," she said. "That's all the papers between Lilly's house and here." Then she spotted her brother's new do. "Good Lord! How desperate are you?" The phone rang, and Mr. Stewart left his bickering kids to answer it.

"Look who's talking!" Jackson shouted, holding up one of the papers Miley had collected. "I'm not the one taking 'Hannah's Wild Ride'! Weeee!"

"Listen, schmohawk, if Lilly finds out why I didn't take her to that party, it'll crush her. I'm not gonna let that happen." Miley was serious. She couldn't stand the thought of hurting Lilly.

Mr. Stewart interrupted. "Then you might want to make those newspapers disappear, because—Lilly in ten."

Miley started running around like a wild woman, scrambling to hide the papers under the couch cushions. "Don't just stand there!" she yelled. "I need tushes! Stat!" She grabbed Jackson and her dad and dragged them over to the couch, where they planted themselves on the goods. Miley ran to the door to intercept Lilly.

"You ready?" Lilly asked Miley when she met her at the door.

Miley was confused. "For what?"

"The mall. I've got to pick out a slammin'

outfit for the next party. I mean, I wouldn't want to embarrass you," Lilly answered.

"Right. Wouldn't want that," Miley said nervously. "Let's go to the mall."

But as they headed for the front door, Jackson spoke up. "The good old mall," he said, "with that big newsstand and all those people talking about what's in the news and who's in the news and—"

Miley took the hint and redirected Lilly, who was still on her skateboard, to the back door. "On the other hand, the beach sounds fun, too," she said.

"But the mall has cute clothes," Lilly protested.

"But the beach has cute boys."

That did it. "To the beach!" Lilly sang.

Miley and Lilly's day at the beach included a stop at the shower platform, where they could watch the cute guys walk by. They were doing just that when Oliver yelled to them.

"Guys!" Oliver yelled. "You'll never guess who made the cover of the entertainment section!" He was waving a newspaper wildly.

Miley had to think fast. She grabbed a football from one of the guys passing by.

"Wait! Oliver, go long!" she shouted, throwing the football as far out of Oliver's reach as she could.

Oliver dove for the ball, shouting, "Too long!" as he fell out of sight.

"Come on, I'm hungry," Miley said to Lilly, dragging her over to the snack counter. But there was no relief anywhere. An old lady sitting next to them was reading a newspaper with the entertainment-section cover face out. Miley grabbed a mustard bottle and squirted it all over the front page of the woman's paper. Lilly noticed what Miley had done, and Miley panicked. She snatched the paper out of the woman's hands and furiously began folding and smashing it. It was a sight to behold.

She looked at the puzzled woman apologetically and said, "There was a bee." She looked at Lilly then. "Big bee," she said to her confused friend. "I think I got it," she said to the woman. A bedraggled Oliver walked over, trading one awkward moment for another. This was getting exhausting for Miley.

"Okay," Oliver panted. "Seriously, I want you guys to see this!" he shouted, still clutching the newspaper.

"Uh . . ." Miley stalled. She noticed a guy carrying a surfboard and got an idea.

"Hey, dude with the board!" she called. The guy turned, just as Miley knew he would, and hit Oliver with the board, sending him flying again. "Never mind!" she yelled to the surfer. "You know what?" she said to Lilly. "It's too crowded here. Hey! Let's go look for sea glass!" The two headed back out to the beach . . . away from all the newspapers!

"Okay," Nina said to Jackson, who was once again sitting in a makeshift barber's chair in the middle of the kitchen. He had a towel wrapped around his head, and Nina was about to unveil her latest attempt. "I think I fixed it. Cross your fingers."

Jackson crossed his fingers, toes, and anything else he could cross as Nina whipped off the towel. "Why do I feel a breeze on my head? Why do I feel my head?" he asked, feeling his newly bald head with his hand. Nina held up a mirror so Jackson could see the result of her work. Meanwhile, Rico watched slyly from the window. "Well, at least I know you're done." Rico heard this, laughed, and walked off feeling mighty satisfied with himself. "But . . . it's okay," Jackson continued. "When it grows back you can try again."

Nina was shocked. "You'd really let me try again?" she asked.

"Sure," Jackson shrugged. "Meanwhile, we could go to a movie . . . where no one can see me."

Nina was exasperated. "I can't take this anymore. You're bald! Why aren't you mad at me?"

"Well, it's not like you did it on purpose," Jackson said.

"But I did!" Nina yelled.

Jackson was floored. "Why? Why would anyone—" Jackson paused, thinking for a minute. Then, a lightbulb went off in his head. "Oh, no, something smells like Rico," he groaned.

"The kid paid me," Nina finally admitted. "I never would've done it if I'd known you were so nice. I just wish I could help you get him back."

"I'm sorry, I'm just too upset to think about revenge right now," Jackson said drearily. He perked up pretty fast, though. "Okay, I'm over it."

The two of them plotted their revenge and headed over to Rico's. Jackson hid nearby while Nina convinced Rico he needed a little haircut of his own. As Jackson had learned, she was pretty convincing! Rico happily obliged and sat down in a chair and let Nina put a smock on him. Rico was so excited about the successful trick he played on Jackson that he had to hear all the details.

"Tell me again what Jackson looked like when he realized it was me," he begged.

Nina made her best frightened face, pretending to mock Jackson's reaction.

"And don't forget the scream," Rico reminded her. "That's my favorite part."

Nina let out a piercing scream.

"Life just doesn't get any better than this," Rico gloated.

"You got it. Just close your eyes, sit back, and relax," Nina told him.

Rico complied, closing his eyes and relaxing to the buzzing sound of Nina's electric hair clippers. What he didn't see was Nina handing her clippers off to Jackson, who had sneaked in and taken over. "Not too much off the sides now," Rico said, eyes still closed.

"Mmm-hmmm," Jackson hummed in as high-pitched a voice as he could.

Chapter Six

It was later that day, much later, when Miley and Lilly got back to the Stewart house. Miley had kept Lilly out collecting sea glass all afternoon and into the evening. It was the only way she could keep her away from the news.

"Wow, I've got enough sea glass to make a coffee table," Miley announced to Lilly. "How about you?"

"I've got enough sea glass to never, ever look for it again," she answered. Then, she noticed a newspaper lying out. "Oh, are the comics here? We didn't get our paper today. Nobody on our block did."

Miley dove over the couch and grabbed the paper out of Lilly's hands. She had gone through too much today to have Lilly find out now. "Oh, who cares about the comics?" she questioned dramatically. "Fat, lazy cats, that pumpkin-headed kid who's always trying to kick the football—boring! Let's just talk—we never talk." She was rambling.

"We talked all day," Lilly said.

"Good point. I'm sick of my own voice." Miley turned on the television. "Let's hear someone else's." But the TV betrayed her.

"Coming up on *This Week in Hollywood*," the voice on the television blared, "*what pouty pop princess pummeled a paparazzi—*" Miley turned the TV off and threw the remote over her shoulder out of Lilly's reach.

"Bad idea!" Miley shouted.

"But I wanted to see that!" Lilly complained. She was distracted, though. She bounced on the couch, noting that something was strange about it. "Why is your couch so lumpy?"

"Ooh! Speaking of lumpy—let's make some oatmeal," Miley suggested, in a misguided attempt to deceive her friend yet again. She dragged Lilly into the kitchen. "Nothing like a big hot bowl of oatmeal after a long day at the beach." Just then, the Hannah line rang, but the phone was nowhere near Miley.

"Ooh, the Hannah phone!" Lilly announced. "Can I get it?"

"No!" Miley yelled.

"Wrong answer!" Lilly said as she

grabbed the phone before Miley could get there. "Hello, Hannah Montana's close personal friend Lola here . . ." Lilly paused to listen. "Oh, my gosh, Kelly!" She covered the phone and looked at Miley. "It's actually Kelly! On your actual phone!" She put on an English accent and returned to the phone. *"Hellooooo . . ."*

"Give me the phone," Miley demanded, chasing Lilly.

But Lilly would not give it up. "So, Kelly-belly, I'm sorry your party was canceled."

"Come on, Lilly," Miley whined nervously, "give it!"

"What do you mean?" Lilly asked Kelly, puzzled. "Hannah said . . ."

Miley was desperate. "Don't listen to her!" she said to Lilly. "She doesn't like me! Professional jealousy! Petty, petty girl!"

Lilly turned to face Miley. "Okay," she said to Kelly somberly, "I'll tell her you called." Then she hung up the phone.

"Lilly," Miley said. "I can explain . . . I didn't tell you about the party because—"

"You didn't want me there," Lilly said.

"No, it wasn't me that didn't want you there, it was . . . everybody else," Miley admitted.

"But, I thought they liked me," Lilly said.

Miley had to tell her the truth now. It was all she had left. "Actually, they thought you were kind of . . . uncool."

"Even after you told them how cool I was?" Lilly saw how guilty Miley looked and realized what was going on. "You didn't tell them, did you?"

"Not exactly," Miley answered.

"Why?" Lilly was hurt.

"It doesn't matter why. You don't need them for friends. Isn't it enough that I'm your friend?" Miley pleaded.

"If you're really my friend, you'll tell me the truth," Lilly reminded her.

"Okay . . ." Miley steeled herself. She knew she had to tell Lilly how she was feeling, but she also knew how hard it would be for her to hear. "You spit food on people, you followed them into bathrooms, and you walked around with a chocolate beard. Lilly . . ." She didn't know what she was going to say next, but Lilly interrupted her, anyway.

"I get it," she said, accepting the blame. "You were embarrassed by me."

"I'm sorry," Miley said. It was all she could say.

"Oh, man, I can't believe I acted like such a dork," Lilly lamented. "Why do I always do that? Lilly, when are you ever gonna learn?" she asked herself out loud as she collapsed onto the couch.

"Don't be so hard on yourself. The first time I saw a chocolate fountain, I got so excited I poured half of it into my purse," Miley reassured her friend.

"You're just saying that to make me feel better." Lilly was onto Miley.

"I know. But—" As she was talking, Lilly pulled a newspaper out from under the couch cushions.

"What's this?" Lilly asked with a puzzled look on her face. She opened the paper to the entertainment section and finally caught a glimpse of the picture Miley had been jumping through hoops to hide all day.

"I kinda got caught leaving the party early," Miley admitted.

"Why were you leaving early?" Lilly asked.

Miley paused and looked at Lilly sweetly. "'Cause it was no fun without you . . . and you know what? That's never gonna happen again."

The next night Miley and Lilly got all dressed up in their Hannah and Lola gear and showed up at the Cobra Room, the club where Traci would be hanging out. As they approached the door, Lilly said, "Miley, I told you, you don't have to do this, we're still best friends."

"Not if I don't do this." Miley was determined to right the wrong she'd done to Lilly. Just then, Traci appeared and approached them.

"Hannah, it's so awesome to see you with . . . her," she said in her snobbiest tone. "What was it again? Lola Loser-Nagle?"

Miley was mad. "It's Luftnagle!" At least she hoped it was. She looked at Lilly. "It *is* Luftnagle, right?"

"I think," Lilly responded with a shrug.

"Well, whatever it is," Traci grumbled, "she's not on the list. Right, Derek?" She looked to the bouncer for backup.

"I don't really care," he said. "Why do people think I care?"

"Because my daddy is the hottest record producer in town," Traci whined.

"Now I care. Can I give you my demo?" Derek asked eagerly as he pulled a CD from his jacket. "It's country."

Traci took the CD from him. "Of course!" she said, faking a smile. "Okay," she said, looking at Hannah, "yes." Then, she turned to Lilly. "No. 'Nuff said."

Lilly pulled away and looked at Miley. "You go, I'll just call my mom."

"No way," Miley commanded. She looked seriously at Traci. "I like you, Trace, but if you wanna be my friend, she's part of the deal."

Traci pulled Miley aside and whispered, "But she's just so uncool."

"Not as uncool as you were when you shot a snot rocket so big it hit the Olsen Twins," she reminded Traci.

Traci was mortified at the memory. "That's not fair. You know I have sinus problems."

"Everybody has problems. But a good friend doesn't bail on you when you have them," Miley lectured. "I didn't bail on you with the twins, and I'm not bailing on Lilly."

"Lola," Lilly volunteered.

"Right," Miley said.

"Okay, fine," Traci conceded, turning toward Lilly. "But, tell anybody about the snot rocket and you're out."

"Deal," Lilly agreed.

"Meet you in there," Traci said to both of them as she headed back inside. Then Miley and Lilly heard a stifled sniffle and turned to see Derek the bouncer wiping away a tear.

"What you did for your friend was real nice," he said to Miley.

"I think so, too," Lilly said to Miley.

Miley couldn't help but blush. "There you go, embarrassing me again." The girls smiled at each other sweetly. Then, the door of the club opened again as a woman exited. Lilly peeked in and caught a glimpse of something . . . or someone that got her going.

"Is that Orlando Bloom?" she yelled. Then, she remembered her vow. "I'm cool. I'm cool," she said . . . coolly.

"Oh, just go for it," Miley said.

"Thanks!" Lilly said, dashing inside.

Derek looked at Miley. "She is kind of a dork."

Miley smiled. "I know. But she's my dork." She headed inside to join Lilly, yelling, "Orlando!" If you can't beat 'em, join 'em. All was well with Miley and Lilly, and it was time to par-*tay*!

Joining 'em was the theme of the evening for Jackson and Rico, too. Back at Rico's, Jackson was fighting off all the snickers about his bald head. His current customer was no exception. He snickered as Jackson handed him a hot dog.

"That's real smart. Laugh at the person

who handles your food!" Jackson shouted, a little worked up.

"You tell 'em, cue ball," Rico said. Rico was sitting there, bald as an eagle as well.

"Thanks, Mini-Me," Jackson said. "You know, I think what we've learned is there are no winners in a war like this. Only hairless casualties."

"You're right," Rico agreed. "Maybe we should call a truce. Deal?"

"Deal," Jackson said.

They each picked up a can of soda, then toasted their new friendship.

"To peace," Rico offered.

"To harmony," Jackson returned. But they both had other plans for each other, as usual. One grabbed a bottle of mustard and the other a bottle of ketchup. It was on! As Jackson and Rico squirted each other, they couldn't help but acknowledge the other's skills in the practical jokes department.

"Touché!" they said in unison. If not the best of friends, they sure were worthy adversaries.

Test your *Hannah Montana* knowledge with this fun quiz!

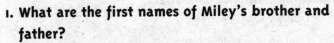

1. **What are the first names of Miley's brother and father?**
   - A. Jordan and Robby
   - B. Jackson and Robby
   - C. Jack and Billy

2. **Who is the first friend Miley tells about her big Hannah Montana secret?**
   - A. Oliver
   - B. Amber
   - C. Lilly

3. **What do Miley and her brother call their grandmother?**
   - A. Ma'maw
   - B. Grandma
   - C. Bubbe

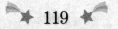

4. Miley's first kiss is shared with which of the following characters?

    A. Oliver

    B. Jake

    C. Josh

5. What career did Miley's dad have before he became Hannah's manager?

    A. He was a singer.

    B. He was a teacher.

    C. He was an actor.

6. Which team do Miley and Lilly try out for together?

    A. Basketball

    B. Track

    C. Cheerleading

7. What name does Lilly use when she goes undercover as Hannah Montana's best friend?

    A. Lala

    B. Lola

    C. Lavender

8. In the first season of Hannah Montana, why does Miley almost tell a reporter about her secret identity?

    A. She wants to be more famous.

    B. She's irritated about Jake Ryan getting treated like a star at school and wishes she could get special treatment, too.

    C. She wants to give the reporter a scoop.

9. When Hannah guest-starred on Jake's TV show, *Zombie High*, what was the name of the character she played?

    A. Miranda, Princess of the Undead

    B. Zaranda, Princess of the Undead

    C. Hannah, Princess of the Undead

10. In order to make Jake jealous, Miley flirts with a boy who she thinks is a senior. What's the boy's name?

    A. Walter

    B. Warren

    C. Willis

11. What grade is the boy she flirts with actually in?

    A. Tenth

    B. Ninth

    C. Eighth

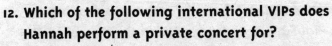

12. **Which of the following international VIPs does Hannah perform a private concert for?**
   A. The Queen of England and her daughter
   B. The King of Spain and his daughter
   C. The Queen of France and her daughter

13. **When Jackson tricks Miley into babysitting for Mr. Dontzig's niece, she ends up taking the girl to a toy store to make a stuffed _____?**
   A. Bear
   B. Moose
   C. Donkey

14. **When Robby gets the flu, which character comes over to the house to take care of him?**
   A. Roxy, Hannah's bodyguard
   B. Mr. Dontzig, the Stewarts' neighbor
   C. Ma'maw, Robby's mom

15. What's the name of Miley and Jackson's aunt, who comes to visit and causes some problems with her video camera?

    A. Molly

    B. Ronnie

    C. Dolly

16. When Miley tries out for the cheerleading squad, she ends up getting the mascot job. What's the mascot of Seaview High School?

    A. A cowboy

    B. A pirate

    C. A bear

ANSWERS:

1. B	5. A	9. B	13. B
2. C	6. C	10. C	14. A
3. A	7. B	11. C	15. C
4. B	8. B	12. A	16. B

SCORING:

Give yourself two points for each correct answer.

If you scored:

0–8
"Nobody's Perfect"

Okay, so you made some mistakes. Well, more than a few. But that's okay. As Hannah's song says, "Nobody's Perfect." Keep watching the show, and we're sure you'll be hitting high notes in no time!

10–20
"Make Some Noise"

Can you hear the crowd cheering for you? That's because you did a fab job! You clearly know a lot about Miley and her friends!

22–32
"This Is the Life"

Kick back and enjoy the moment, because this is the life! You are a *Hannah Montana* whiz!

Face-off

Adapted by Alice Alfonsi

Based on the series created by Michael Poryes and Rich Correll & Barry O'Brien

Part One is based on the episode, "You're So Vain, You Probably Think This Zit Is About You," Written by Todd J. Greenwald

Part Two is based on the episode, "Ooo, Ooo Itchy Woman," Written by Steven Peterman & Gary Dontzig

New York

PART ONE

Chapter One

"**W**onderful, Hannah! Brilliant!" exclaimed Liza, behind her high-priced camera. The tall, stylish woman ran one of the top photography studios in the business. And her job today was simple — capture pop-singing sensation Hannah Montana on film.

For over an hour, Miley Stewart had been trying hard to look hip, hot, and Hannah-ish. Beneath her blond wig and sunglasses, she was totally working it. But, boy, was she tired of smiling!

While Hannah struck pose after pose in her glittery clothes, her dad stood a few feet away. With his big arms folded, he quietly watched the photo shoot behind his usual disguise—a huge fake mustache, long-haired wig, and baseball cap.

"You look gorgeous, radiant," Liza told Hannah. In the background, the studio's sound system pounded out Hannah's latest hit.

"This is the life," the photographer squawked along with the song. "Hold on tight. . . ."

Hannah's beaming smile suddenly fell. She couldn't help it. Liza may have been a talented photographer, but she was one lousy singer.

"Stop, stop, stop!" Liza cried, seeing Hannah's expression go sour. "Darling," she scolded, "we're doing an ad for skin cream, not wart removal! What *is* that face?"

Mr. Stewart stepped forward. "I think it's a reaction to your *singin'*," he drawled.

Hannah burst out laughing. But Liza was not amused. She narrowed her eyes on the strapping man in sunglasses. "And *you* are?" she asked pointedly.

"Hannah's manager," he replied, keeping it simple.

"Well, *Hannah's manager*," Liza rudely snapped, "I'm an award-winning photographer, so why don't you just push your tush *off* my set."

Mr. Stewart frowned. Clearly, the woman needed a little more information. "I'm also her *father*," he informed her.

Liza blinked in surprise. Then she turned to her photography assistant. "I need a chair for Mr. Montana's tush!" she shouted. "Now!"

The young man quickly brought over a chair. Mr. Stewart sat.

"Comfy?" Liza asked, her voice suddenly sweet as honey.

Mr. Stewart grinned. "Like a monkey in a banana bath."

Liza pictured that idea and shuddered. "How charming." She wheeled back to face Hannah. "Okay, now, Hannah, darling, Magic Glow skin cream, everyone's favorite zit zapper, is using this billboard to launch a worldwide campaign. So give me *jubilance* peppered with *rapture* and sprinkle it with a dash of *je ne sais quoi*."

Say *what*? Hannah thought, scrunching her face up in total confusion.

"No, no, no, that's not even close," complained Liza.

Hannah sighed. "Well, if you lighten up on the SAT words, it might help."

Now the photographer was the one who looked confused. So, Mr. Stewart suppressed a chuckle and gave her a clue. "How 'bout, 'Say cheese'?"

Liza shouted over her shoulder, "I need some *cheese* for Mr. Montana!"

Mr. Stewart shook his head. "Slow down, there," he drawled as he moseyed over to the photographer. "All I'm saying is, you might get a little more out of Hannah if you just keep it simple."

"Yes, Mr. Montana, anything you say," Liza replied through a stiff smile. Then she turned to her assistant and whispered, "Just what I need. Jethro's chicken-fried wisdom."

With a sigh, Liza looked through her viewfinder again. "Okay, Hannah . . ." she declared, "say *cheese*!"

Hannah took a deep breath. She knew

what the photographer wanted, but she was so tired of posing and smiling that it wasn't easy.

Just then, she noticed her dad doing something right behind the photographer. As the Hannah Montana music played in the background, her dad began to dance — really badly.

Hannah laughed. Her happy expression was genuine and beautiful. It was that million dollar look Liza had been waiting for.

"Perfection!" she cried, snapping away. "I've done it again!"

Chapter Two

The next morning, Miley and her buds were hanging at Rico's, a snack shack near the beach. In the back of the joint was a basketball court. And Miley joined a group of kids for a pickup game.

"You want it, try and get it," Miley challenged. She was dribbling down the court when Donny stepped in front of her.

When she couldn't get around the tall jock, he laughed in her face. "Come on," he taunted. "It's like taking candy from a baby."

Miley shook her head, looking defeated. Then she pointed to his pants. "Your zipper's down."

When Donny glanced down to check, Miley cried, "Oliver!" And she passed the ball to him.

Danny spun, but Oliver was already dribbling toward the basket for a shot.

"Look out! Heads up!" Lilly cried.

Oliver was about to shoot when Lilly crashed right into him. Both of them fell to the ground.

"Come on, man, flagrant foul!" Oliver complained.

Lilly rose to her feet, looking guilty. "Sorry. My bad," she admitted.

She picked up the ball and moved to pass it back to Oliver. But she didn't appear to see him. Instead, she walked over to the basketball pole.

"Here you go," she told the pole. She held out the ball and let it go. The ball dropped to the ground.

"Nice hands, Shaq," she quipped.

Okay, thought Miley, enough is enough. She pulled her best girlfriend off the court and into the snack shack. "Lilly, why aren't you wearing your contacts?"

Lilly sighed, looking dejected. "My dog ate 'em," she admitted, "along with an entire tube of toothpaste. He's been doing *this* all morning—" Lilly licked her teeth, then stuck out her tongue.

Miley laughed. "Well, that's more toothpaste than my brother's used in his entire life."

Miley's older brother worked behind Rico's counter. And he'd just overheard her insult.

"What a h-h-h-h-orrible thing to say,"

Jackson told his sister, exhaling his stinky breath all over her.

Miley held her nose and waved her hand. "Thanks for proving my point," she told him. Then she turned back to Lilly. "How are you going to sneak a peek at my billboard tonight if you can't *see* it?"

Lilly shrugged. "I'll just imagine your head really big with pigeons on it."

Miley frowned and crossed her arms.

"I know you're giving me a look," said Lilly. "I just can't see it."

Miley rolled her eyes. "Don't you have backup glasses?"

"Oh, you mean these?" Lilly pulled out her glasses and put them on.

Miley tried to hide her shock. The glasses were huge, clunky, and uglier than a hairy wart. But Lilly was her best friend, and she didn't want to hurt her feelings.

"Wow . . . wee!" Miley said, stalling to think of what to say about the dorky goggles. "Look at those . . . uh, *stylin'* specs!"

"Nice try," Lilly said flatly, then shook her head in despair. "Never let your mother buy you glasses at a place that also sells tires."

"Hey, Truscott!" cried a tough-looking skater girl.

"Oh, no," Lilly whispered to Miley. "It's Heather."

Heather was Lilly's skateboarding rival. Both girls had been competing against each other since they'd learned to skate. Now Heather was striding across Rico's floor like she owned the place. As usual, her little sidekick, Kim, was trailing close behind.

Seeing the two girls coming, Lilly whipped off her glasses and hid them fast.

"Congrats on making the half-pipe

finals," Heather told Lilly with a smile. Then she grimaced. "I'm so sorry."

"About what?" Lilly asked.

"Sorry I'm going to beat you," Heather replied. "Again."

"Beat you again!" Kim repeated.

"You've got no chance," Heather declared.

"No chance!" Kim echoed.

Heather glanced at Kim. "Shut up!"

"Shut up!" Kim started to say, then realized that last comment was meant for her. "Oh."

"You're the one who's got no chance," Lilly replied. Unfortunately, without her glasses, she went nose to nose with Kim instead of Heather.

"Okay, that's it," said Miley, stepping up for her bud. "Listen, slick," she told Heather. "No one talks to my girl like that.

And Saturday night in the finals, you're going down! You may have beaten Lilly last year, and the year before, and the year—"

"I think she gets it!" Lilly interjected.

Heather turned to Lilly. "You're the one who's going to get it bad."

"Get it baaaaaad!" repeated little Kim. Then she noticed Heather giving her a *you're getting tiresome* look. "Too much?"

"You think?" Heather spat. Then she turned on her trainers and stomped away with Kim right on her heels.

"You may be the *champion* now," Miley called after her, "but after Saturday, you're going to be the *chumpion*!" She turned to Lilly. "High five."

Miley raised her hand and Lilly swung to slam it. But Lilly missed her best friend's hand and struck her forehead instead.

"Ow!" cried Miley.

Just then, Lilly's cell phone rang.

"Please, answer your phone," said Miley, rubbing her head, "before you hurt somebody else."

Lilly pulled out her phone and answered. "Hello. Hi, Mom . . . what?! . . . but they said . . ." Lilly listened some more, but the news was obviously bad. "Okay, bye," she finally said.

Miley waited for an explanation.

"My contacts aren't coming in till next week," Lilly informed her.

"Big deal," Miley replied with a shrug. "You'll just wear your glasses to the finals. Who cares?"

"I do!" Lilly cried. "No way I'm going to compete if I have to wear these."

"Are you kidding me?" Miley exclaimed. "All you've been talking about is you're going to double kick-flip Heather all over that skate park this year."

"That was with two eyes, not four," countered Lilly. "I'm not going in front of all those people looking like this."

Miley threw up her hands. "Will you forget about how you look? It's what's on the inside that counts."

Lilly folded her arms. "Easy for you to say. You're the poster child for perfect skin."

"This isn't about me," Miley replied. "Or my perfect skin." Just then, she spotted Oliver at the counter, buying a taco from her brother. "Hey, Oliver, would you please tell Lilly that looks don't matter?"

"Okay," he said, wandering over. "Looks don't matter."

Miley turned back to Lilly. "See? If Oliver can say that with his nostril thing, you can get over your glasses."

"Yeah," Oliver agreed. Then he froze. "What?"

"You know," Miley told Oliver, "how one is way bigger than the other."

Oliver stared at her dumbfounded.

Miley turned back to Lilly. "But you don't see him obsessing over it."

Oliver immediately grabbed a stainless steel napkin dispenser. He examined his reflection in the shiny surface.

"Look at me!" he howled. "I'm a lopsided freak!"

Miley frowned. "I'm sorry, I thought you knew."

Totally disturbed, Oliver headed home. As he crossed the beach dunes, he passed some sunbathers who innocently glanced his way.

Oliver didn't think it was so innocent.

"Stop staring at me!" he shrieked. "I'm not an animal!"

The sunbathers just scratched their heads in confusion as Oliver raced away.

Chapter Three

That afternoon, Miley's father was unloading the dishwasher in the kitchen.

"Plate, cup, bowl," he recited to himself. "Glass, pot, underwear . . . What the —?"

He stared at the neon-colored briefs. No way they were his. Or Miley's. That left only one other person.

"Jackson," Mr. Stewart muttered. "There's something wrong with that boy."

Just then, the front door opened. And

Mr. Stewart looked up to find his teenage son dragging in.

"Why?" Jackson griped. "Why me? Why?"

"I was asking myself that *same* question not five seconds ago," Mr. Stewart told him, "when I unloaded *these*."

Mr. Stewart held up the underwear—stretched out across a dinner plate, no less. Jackson rushed over to check it out.

"Whoa, it worked!" he cried excitedly. "They're clean again—"

Mr. Stewart slung the briefs into his son's face.

"—and lemon fresh!" Jackson happily added.

"On the bright side," said Mr. Stewart, "I'm glad to see you're *wearing* underwear again."

Jackson nodded.

"So," said Mr. Stewart, "how did your date go?"

"I still can't believe it. I finally got Jill to go out with me, we're cruising down the coastal highway, I did that yawn thing, got my arm around her. And then . . ." Jackson made a raspberry noise.

Mr. Stewart cringed. "Well, I can see where that could be embarrassing. At least you were in a convertible."

"Dad, it wasn't *me*," Jackson said. "It was the car! I didn't have enough money to fill it up and I ran out of gas. It was *humiliating*."

"Don't sweat it, Son," said Mr. Stewart. "I'm sure your friend understood. It's not like you made her get out and push."

"Well, actually . . ." Jackson began. But he was interrupted when the front door opened.

In came Jackson's date. Jill was a pretty sixteen-year-old, but at the moment she looked a total wreck. After pushing Jackson's car down the coastal highway, she was sweaty, dirty, exhausted—and *really* unhappy.

"This has been the worst date of my entire life!" she exclaimed.

Jackson tried to look sympathetic. He walked over to her and grinned. "Maybe a little kiss will make it better?"

Jill slammed down the bill of Jackson's cap, then stomped back out the door.

Mr. Stewart couldn't believe his son had treated his date like a pack mule. He glared at his boy. But Jackson felt completely justified.

"Well, somebody had to steer," he said defensively.

* * *

The next day, Jackson was back working behind the counter at Rico's.

"Here you go, sir," he said, handing a customer his order. "Nice, cold bottle of water. And your change . . . which I'm putting right next to the conveniently located *tip jar*."

Actually, it would have been really hard for the man to miss the tip jar. There was a big, red, flashing neon sign right in front of it that read TIPS!

"And, may I say," Jackson added in a syrupy sweet voice, "that's a very handsome shirt."

But when the customer took his change and departed without leaving so much as a buffalo nickel, Jackson's sweet voice turned sour. "And about that shirt —my grandma's got a couch just like it!"

Jackson started to consider a *bigger* neon sign for the jar, when a dark-haired kid wandered over.

"Hello . . . *Jackson*," said the kid with venom.

"Hello . . . *Rico*," Jackson replied with equal venom.

"So," Rico began, "your boss—the man I call *Daddy*—tells me you asked him for a raise?"

"Yeah, I did," Jackson replied. "Girls like cars, cars like gas, and gas costs money. What's it to you?"

"Well, *Daddy* still hasn't made up his mind," Rico informed him. "Could go either way. If only you had someone on the *inside*. Someone who knows how to pull on his heartstrings and make him dance like a little puppet."

Jackson rolled his eyes. Rico was

obviously referring to himself. "What do you want, Rico?"

Rico's reply was a slow, sly smile.

"And now," Rico announced an hour later, "the Great Ricolini will perform the legendary disappearing egg trick!"

Rico was standing on the beach behind his father's fast-food shack. He was dressed in a black cape and top hat, and holding a magic wand. A small crowd had gathered to watch his act.

"I'll just need the help of my charming assistant," he told the crowd, "the lovely Tina!"

Hearing his introduction, Jackson stepped out of the girls' bathroom. He was decked out in the costume Rico had given him—a glittery gold dress with a short skirt and long, white gloves.

I can't believe I agreed to this, Jackson thought. Apparently, Rico had been fantasizing about doing a magic act for months. All he needed was a female assistant. The only problem was—he couldn't find any females willing to help him out. Now Jackson was stuck pretending to be "the lovely Tina."

Carrying a velvet pillow with an egg on it, Jackson moved to stand beside Rico the Magician. As soon as he got there, Rico nudged Jackson to remind him about the speech they'd rehearsed.

"Here, oh Great Ricolini," Jackson recited flatly. "The magical egg. Please, no flash photography."

"Isn't she wonderful?" Rico declared to the crowd. Then he whispered to Jackson, "Come on, Tina, work it."

Jackson didn't move. Rico rubbed his

fingers in the universal sign for cash. And Jackson reluctantly struck a sexy pose.

Rico grinned. He took the egg from Jackson's pillow and addressed the crowd. "I hold in my hand what looks to be an ordinary egg. . . . But is it?"

He smashed the egg on Jackson's head. "Yes, it is!" Rico cried.

The crowd screamed with laughter, and Rico bowed.

"And I thank you!" he told them.

Jackson wanted to strangle the kid. But then he pictured his car without gasoline and himself without a date.

I had *better* get a raise out of this, Jackson told himself as yolk dripped down his face. Or I'll be making the Great Ricolini disappear.

Chapter Four

"**L**illy, there's no one up here!" Miley cried, later that night. "This is really getting stupid."

Miley's father huffed and puffed as he carried Lilly the last few steps to the roof. "Oh, we passed *stupid* on the third floor," he grumbled. "Now we're up to *sports hernia*."

Miley was desperate to check out the big Hannah billboard. And she wanted her best friend to see it, too. But Lilly had refused to wear her dorky glasses in public.

And without her glasses, she couldn't *see* the steps they had to climb. So, Mr. Stewart carried Lilly all the way up, piggyback style.

"Okay, fine," said Lilly. Mr. Stewart set her down on the rooftop, and she put on her glasses. "Wow!" she exclaimed, finally able to see. "This is cool up here!" Then she noticed Miley staring at her.

"What?" Lilly demanded.

"You know, those glasses really don't look that bad," she said sincerely.

"You're not just saying that?" Lilly asked with a flicker of hope. "They really look okay?"

Miley nodded. "Good enough to beat Heather at the skate finals."

Lilly thought it over. "Well . . ." she said.

Mr. Stewart could see the girl needed more convincing. "If it helps you," he told her, "I think they're pretty cool."

Lilly's hopeful expression crumbled. "Aw, man!" she exclaimed, throwing up her hands.

Mr. Stewart looked at Miley in total confusion. "What?" he asked.

"She was *this* close!" Miley whispered, holding two fingers an inch apart. "I almost had her!"

Mr. Stewart still didn't follow. "What'd I say?"

Miley sighed. "Dad, when a parent says something's cool, you *know* it's dorky."

"Okay, I get it," Mr. Stewart told Miley. Then he turned once more to face his daughter's best friend. "Lilly," he said sincerely, "the truth is, those glasses are a big bowl of ugly."

Lilly gasped. "Thanks a lot!"

Miley couldn't believe her dad. *Now* her

best friend was near tears. She turned to her clueless father and cried, "Why don't you just push her off the roof?!"

Mr. Stewart massaged his temples. The pain in his back was nothing compared to this! "You girls sure were easier when you were eight," he griped. "I'd say, 'That's a pretty dress.' And you'd say, 'Thank you, Mr. Stewart.'"

Miley rolled her eyes, and Mr. Stewart clapped his hands and declared, "Okay, enough chitchat. Let's have a look at this thing."

He walked to the side of the big billboard. A tarp still covered it, and he began to yank it off.

Miley turned her back on the billboard. She was still worried about her bestie. "Lilly, trust me," she said, gripping her friend's shoulder. "When you beat Heather, no one's going to be looking at your glasses. They're going to be looking at that big trophy in your hand."

Lilly thought it over. "It *is* big, isn't it?"

"Oh, yeah," said Miley. "And if this were me, I wouldn't let how I *look* stop me from going after it."

"Really?" Lilly's eyes opened wide, but not because of what Miley had said. Mr. Stewart had just finished uncovering the Hannah Montana billboard. And Lilly couldn't believe what was sitting on her friend's twenty-foot-high face.

"What if you had a zit the size of an extra-large pizza?" Lilly asked.

Miley waved her hand. "Come on. Now you're just being ridiculous."

"Oh, yeah?" said Lilly. "Turn around."

Miley spun and saw the uncovered billboard. Hannah's million dollar smile was right there from the photo shoot. But so was something else—something that hadn't been there the day of the shoot. A large, ugly zit had been added to her forehead. The slogan on the ad read: *Even I get zits*.

"Holy zit!" Miley cried.

Her father was also stunned. "Man," he said, "that thing's big enough to have its own chairlift!"

"Chairlift?" said Lilly. "It's big enough to have its own zit code!"

Miley folded her arms. "Why don't I just wait in the car till you're done making fun of me?!"

"Sorry, Mile," said her dad. "Don't worry, I'm going to find out what's going on. This has to be a mistake. A big, red, blotchy—"

"That's it!" Miley cried. "I'm going to the car!"

As soon as they got home, Miley's dad called the photographer. Unfortunately, the conversation didn't go very well.

". . . No, ma'am. No way," said Mr. Stewart, trying to control his anger. "We never agreed to something like this."

"I know, but I had an inspiration," Liza replied on the other end of the phone line.

The stylish woman was in the middle of a photo shoot. She wore a hands-free head-set as she moved around her studio, taking pictures of her latest subject.

"What inspiration?" asked Mr. Stewart.

Liza shrugged. "If Hannah Montana says, 'Even I get zits,' she should *have* a zit. It was staring me right in the face."

Mr. Stewart gripped the phone tighter. "Now it's staring *Los Angeles* right in the face, and we don't like it."

"I hear your concerns," Liza cooed, trying to smooth Mr. Stewart's ruffled feathers. "Believe me, there's nothing more important to me right now than your feelings—uh, be right back!"

Liza crossed her studio and approached her photographic subject. "I need more emotion!" she told him. "You're running through a meadow! The sun is shining. You're happy. You're in love!"

For a moment, the sad old hound dog just sat there in his superhero cape, listening to Liza's direction. Then he yawned and began to howl.

Liza threw up her hands. "I can't work with this!"

While Mr. Stewart waited for Liza to return to their conversation, he wandered outside, to the beach house deck.

Lilly and Miley remained in the living

room, talking. Well, *actually*, Lilly was talking. Miley was moping.

"So," said Lilly, "not so easy when it's *your* face that has a problem."

Miley knew that Lilly was right. Unless she wanted to look like a hypocrite, she had to pretend the zit was okay.

"I don't have a problem," Miley told her best friend. "Why should I have a problem? After all, looks don't matter. And if that's the way they want to go with this *worldwide* campaign, I'll be fine with it."

Just then, her dad came back inside. "Sorry, sweetheart," he said, "but that's the way they want to go with this *worldwide* campaign."

What!? Miley wanted to scream. But Lilly was staring right at her, so instead she said, "Really? Great . . . terrific . . . awesome! I love it!"

Mr. Stewart scratched his head. "You do?"

"Yes, I *do*," she pointedly told her dad. Then she turned back to Lilly. "When I say, 'Looks don't matter,' I mean it. Because I don't just talk the talk, I walk the walk."

Lilly's eyebrows rose. "You are amazing. I mean, if you can stand up in front of the whole world with that *ginormous* zit, something any normal person would be humiliated by—"

Miley squirmed. "Get to the point, Lilly."

"The point is," Lilly said, "if you can do all that, I can wear my glasses to that skate competition."

Miley was floored. Wow, she thought. I did it. I actually convinced Lilly to wear her glasses.

"Thank you so much," Lilly said, hugging Miley tight. 'This is the greatest thing

you've ever done for me. I am going to double kick-flip Heather all over that skate
park! Thanks to you."

Miley remained speechless as she
watched her best friend head out the door.
Mr. Stewart crossed over to his daughter
and put an arm around her. "I'm proud of
ya, Mile," he said.

But Mr. Stewart might not be so proud
when he found out what Miley was plan-
ning to do next.

Chapter Five

The next day didn't get any better for Jackson Stewart.

"And for my next trick," Rico announced, "the Great Ricolini will make the tempting Tina disappear!"

Jackson was back in his gold dress and white gloves. Just like the day before, Rico had attracted a small crowd near the back of his father's beachfront snack shack. Now the kid was gesturing for Jackson to squeeze into a cage.

"Tina?" Rico prompted.

Jackson stared at the little cage. He wanted a raise, but this is where he drew the line. "Ain't gonna happen," he told Rico.

Rico smiled, pulled out a twenty-dollar bill and dropped it inside the cage. "Fetch," he said.

Okay, thought Jackson, so I'm a dude with no shame. He climbed in after the twenty.

"Go get it, Tina," Rico taunted. "Good girl."

He shut the cage door tight and turned to the audience. "Now watch closely as I make Tina disappear!" He covered the cage with a blanket and waved his wand. "One. Two . . ."

The Great Ricolini never got to *three*. Instead, he turned to two men in courier outfits. "Okay, boys!" he cried. "Take it away!"

The first courier stepped up. "Where's this going, kid?"

Rico grinned. "San Diego Zoo. And don't feed him, he bites."

"Ricoooooooooo!" Jackson cried as the two couriers wheeled him away.

But Rico wasn't listening. He was too busy taking his bow. "And I thank you," he told his applauding audience.

By that night, Jackson was free again— and on a top secret mission. He and Miley had dressed in black from head to toe. Together they climbed to the roof of the building where the Hannah Montana billboard was located.

"Come on, Jackson," whispered Miley. She waved at her brother from the billboard's catwalk. "We've got to do this fast."

Jackson didn't move a muscle. He just stood on the rooftop, holding the roller and bucket of paint. "Sorry," he told his sister, "I need my cash up front. I've got one kid yanking my chain already. I don't need another."

"Fine." Miley slapped a ten-dollar bill onto his waiting palm. "Half now and half when you complete the job."

"Done," said Jackson. He pocketed the cash, then moved to the catwalk and removed the tarp covering the billboard.

"Whoa," he said, checking out the giant zit. "I hope we brought enough paint."

Miley was about to tell him what he could do with his paint, when the roar of a helicopter interrupted her. A chopper swooped right toward them. Its spotlight swept the area.

"Snap! It's *the man*!" Miley freaked and grabbed her brother's arm. "Do they allow makeup in prison?"

"It's just a traffic chopper," Jackson replied. "Stay out of the light."

Miley and Jackson jumped off the catwalk. They dodged the sweeping beam and hid in a shadowy corner of the rooftop.

A minute later, the helicopter's spotlight swept the billboard and froze on Hannah's forehead. The pilot's voice came over the helicopter's loudspeaker.

"Bill," he said, "check out the size of that zit. I think we found the cause of the traffic jam."

Miley jumped up in outrage. "Hey!"

"Get down!" Jackson warned, pulling her back into the shadows.

After the helicopter left, Miley and Jackson moved back onto the catwalk. Miley grabbed the paint roller and climbed onto her brother's shoulders.

"What are you going to tell Lilly at the big unveiling when she sees the zit is gone?" Jackson asked.

"Not a problem," said Miley, working the roller. "She'll be at the skateboard competition. By the time she sees this, she'll have her trophy, and I'll have my face back. . . ." With a final flourish, she finished making her zit—and her problem—disappear. "Just . . . like . . . that."

"Nice work," called a deep voice.

"Thanks," Miley replied. "You know, sometimes that voice in my head sounds exactly like Dad."

"There's a reason for that," said the deep voice.

Miley and Jackson turned to see who'd just spoken.

"Snap! It's *the man*!" Miley cried for

the second time that night.

Mr. Stewart put his hands on his hips. "Nothing makes me happier than seein' my kids doing chores together. So, who was the mastermind behind this operation?"

"Okay," said Miley with a *you-caught-me* shrug. "Jackson made me do it."

"What?" Jackson cried.

By now, brother and sister were back on the roof again, standing beside their dad. Miley noticed a paintbrush sticking out of her father's pocket.

"Hey, Dad," she said. "Why do you have a paintbrush?"

"Okay," said Mr. Stewart with his own *you-caught-me* shrug. "Jackson made me do it."

"What?!" Jackson cried.

Mr. Stewart turned to his daughter. "Mile, you know I'll always be there for you. You're my little girl."

Father and daughter hugged. And Jackson folded his arms. "Hey," he said, tapping his dad's shoulder. "What am I?"

Mr. Stewart shrugged. "Tina. My other little girl."

The next morning, Jackson was back at Rico's snack shack, working hard behind the counter. The Great Ricolini strode up and plopped onto a stool.

Jackson smiled at the kid. "So, Rico," he said, "check this out." He pointed to three coconut shells sitting on the counter. He lifted one to show Rico that a red ball sat underneath.

"What's this?" Rico asked.

"Your little magic act inspired me," Jackson said. "Keep your eye on the ball." He covered up the red ball again and began to shuffle the coconuts. "It goes round and round. The amazing works of Jacksoni! Now, where's the ball?".

"Nice try, amateur," Rico scoffed. He lifted the correct coconut, revealing the red ball. "You call that a trick?"

"No," said Jackson. "I call that a *setup*. Here's the trick." Jackson reached up and pulled on a rope. A bucket, rigged above Rico, turned over and poured seaweed all over the kid's head.

Rico grimaced at the briny, wet mess.

Ha! Jackson thought. Payback is always so *sweet*. "You want this?" he asked, holding out a towel. "Fetch."

Jackson threw the towel across the snack shack and Rico took off after it.

"Your dad called me this morning," Jackson called after Rico. "I got the raise." With a grin, the Great Jacksoni bowed. "And I thank you."

Rico furiously grit his teeth. "This isn't over," he promised, stomping back with the towel.

But it was over for Jackson. He started dancing around. "I got the *ra-aise*," he sang, "and dumped that *o-on* you—"

"Jackson?" a pretty girl interrupted.

It was Jill, Jackson's date from the other day—the one who'd pushed his car all the way home.

"Jill! Good news!" Jackson exclaimed. "I'm a man with money! And a lot of gas." When she gave him a funny look, he clarified. ". . . In my *car*."

"What did you do to this little boy?" Jill demanded, pointing at Rico.

"First of all," said Jackson, "he's not a little boy."

But Rico's eyes were already glimmering with an evil idea. "I want my mommy!" Rico cried.

"Stop that!" Jackson demanded.

"No, you stop," Rico whined. He stuck his thumb in his mouth and turned to Jill. "Make him stop, nice lady."

Jill patted Rico on the head. She turned and glared at Jackson. "And to think I was coming over here to give you a second chance," she scolded.

"But—" Jackson began.

Jill turned back to Rico. "It's okay," she cooed.

"He's the devil!" Jackson blurted out.

"And you're pathetic," Jill replied. Then she took Rico's hand. "Come on, sweetie, I'll take you home and wash you off."

Rico continued his fake sobs as Jill led him away. "I prefer sponge baths," he informed her as Jackson whimpered.

"But . . . but . . . I have money," Jackson

called, pulling out his wallet and waving the cold, hard cash.

Unfortunately, it no longer mattered. With one last evil smile, the Great Ricolini just made Jackson's date disappear.

Chapter Six

Later that day was the official unveiling of Hannah's billboard. A podium and microphone had been set up on the rooftop. And a crowd gathered to watch the famous Liza talk about her latest work.

Miley arrived with her dad. Both were wearing their Montana disguises. Miley had on her blond Hannah wig, cool sunglasses, and pop-star clothes. And her dad was dressed in his "manager's" outfit, complete with big mustache, long hair, and baseball cap.

Together, father and daughter made their way past two large security guards, a group of press photographers, and a number of important guests.

Liza was in the middle of the crowd, preening like a peacock. "Who wants to talk to me?" she loudly asked. "Oh, hi!" she said to a young local reporter, then changed her mind and shoved him away. "No, you're not important enough."

Suddenly, she spotted Hannah and her father arriving. "Ah, it's the Montana posse," she said, walking over to them. "*Howdy*. And once again, I am sorry about . . . what *was* I sorry about?"

Miley's father crossed his arms. "Putting that zit on my child's forehead without our permission," he reminded her.

Liza stiffened. "Right, well . . ." She inched away, glancing around. "Who *else* wants to talk to me?"

Just then, Hannah heard a "Pssst!" She turned to see Lilly waving at her. A burly security guard had stopped her at the door, and she was trying to get Hannah's attention.

Omigosh, thought Hannah. She exchanged a worried look with her father. *Why* is Lilly here?!

Her father just shrugged.

Hannah faced the door again. She waved to the guard to allow Lilly inside.

"Lilly, what are you doing here?" Hannah asked when her friend bounded over. "You're *supposed* to be at the skateboard competition."

Lilly nodded. "I'm going straight from here."

She opened her long coat to show off her colorful spandex skater wear, with matching knee and elbow pads. Her helmet was in the backpack slung over her shoulder. And she was already wearing her big, dorky glasses.

She shrugged. "What kind of friend would I be if I didn't come to support you after all you did for me?"

Hannah gulped. "That is so sweet. Thank you so much . . . now *go*."

"No, no, no," Lilly insisted. "When they pull that cover off and expose that big zit, I'm going to be right here for you."

"Again," Hannah said. "*Appreciate* it, now *go*."

"Ladies and gentlemen," Liza announced at the podium.

Uh-oh, Hannah thought. The presentation's *starting*! And Lilly isn't *leaving*!

"I'd like to present my latest master-piece," Liza continued. "The worldwide premiere of the Magic Glow skin cream campaign!"

Liza pulled the cord, and the tarp fell away. She gestured proudly to the sign, then realized something was missing.

"Where is her zit?" Liza murmured, totally confused.

Lilly was confused, too. She stared up at Hannah's face. "Hey, what happened to the zit?" she asked Hannah. "Where'd it go?"

Hannah gulped, trying to think of an explanation. "Wow!" she finally cried. "That zit cream is *good*!"

The photographer wasn't buying it. She just kept staring at the billboard. Then a thought occurred to her, and she turned to glare at Mr. Stewart.

"Where's my zit?" Liza loudly demanded. "I loved that zit!"

Mr. Stewart didn't flinch. "That'll teach you to sell us a horse and deliver a mule."

That's when it hit Lilly. She wheeled on Hannah. "You covered it up!" she cried.

"Lilly," Hannah pleaded, "you don't understand."

"Oh, I understand fine," Lilly shot back. "You *lied* to me. All that stuff about 'Looks don't matter, it's what's on the inside'—you never meant a word of it."

"Yes, I did . . . until it was my face," Hannah admitted. "Look, just because I couldn't take my own advice doesn't mean you shouldn't! Go to that skateboard competition. Teach me a lesson. Be my role model."

Lilly snapped her fingers. "Save it," she told Hannah, tearing off her dorky glasses.

"Why should I believe anything you tell me?"

"Because . . ." Hannah said, thinking fast, "you said it was the best thing I ever did for you."

"Well . . ." Lilly replied, "sometimes I say things I don't mean. *You* should know what *that's* like."

Hannah couldn't believe it. Lilly was furious and now she was leaving. "Lilly—"

Hannah crossed the roof to stop Lilly, but she had to walk right by Liza at the podium. And the angry photographer wasn't about to let Hannah Montana get away clean.

"Well, here she is," Liza announced into the microphone, "the new Magic Glow skin girl . . . Miss Can't-Even-Have-One-Li'l-Blemish-No-Matter-How-Many-Awards-I'd-Win-If-She-Did."

Hannah tried to get by, but Liza grabbed

her arm. "Ladies and gentlemen," Liza cried, "Hannah Montana!"

Stuck at the podium, Hannah signaled the security guard by the door. "Don't let her go," she demanded, pointing to Lilly.

The big guard nodded and blocked Lilly's path. Lilly was a pretty good dodge artist, but this guy was a rock. And without her glasses on, she just couldn't get by him.

Meanwhile, as Hannah moved to the microphone, the crowd applauded. "Thank you," she said. "It's a real honor to be a spokesperson for Magic Glow skin cream. And if I've learned anything from this experience, it's that nobody's perfect, even celebrities."

"You look pretty perfect up there," Lilly angrily shouted by the door.

Hannah felt terrible. This is stupid, she thought. And it's totally not worth losing my best friend. But what can I do?

Spying a pitcher of water on the podium, Hannah got an idea. She took the pitcher in her hand. "Yeah, sometimes I do look pretty perfect," Hannah admitted. "But sometimes, I look like this—"

With one grand toss, she threw the pitcher of water onto the billboard. The water splashed on the sign and washed the paint away from the giant zit.

The photographer happily clapped her hands, and the crowd began to murmur.

Curious, Lilly put her glasses back on. "Whoa," she whispered, seeing what Hannah had done.

Mr. Stewart looked up at the billboard, then down at his daughter—and smiled proudly.

Hannah shrugged. "I didn't want people

seeing me that way," she confessed to the crowd, "but I was wrong." She met Lilly's *four* eyes. "Looks aren't everything. . . . I mean, I'm not going to say they don't matter, but there's a lot of stuff that matters more. And if you let a zit or, say, *dorky glasses*, stop you from living your life, you're going to regret it. You really will."

Hannah held her breath, waiting to see what Lilly would do. She didn't have to wait long. Lilly gave her best friend a huge thumbs-up.

Hannah grinned. "So take your pictures," she told the crowd. "Let the world see that even Hannah Montana has zits." She gestured to her billboard. "And I'm okay with it."

Just then, a fluttering shadow crossed Hannah's face.

PLOP!

Miley sighed. A bird had left its sticky white calling card on her shoulder. *Gross*, she thought. Zits are one thing, but . . . "*This*," she admitted, "I ain't so crazy about."

Sheesh, Miley thought. I never knew life as a superstar would be so hard!

PART TWO

Chapter One

The lipstick came out of nowhere.

Well, actually, it came out of Amber's designer handbag. She passed it to her best friend, Ashley, who slathered it all over Oliver Oken's mouth.

Oliver never saw it coming—mainly because his eyes were closed. He had nodded off at his desk while waiting for class to start.

"Oh, yeah, baby," Oliver murmured as Ashley painted his lips a stylin' shade of bubble gum pink.

Kids gathered around Oliver's desk and snickered. Oliver didn't hear them. Beneath his shaggy dog bangs, he remained happily in dreamland.

"I love you, too," he mumbled.

Ashley tossed her long, dark hair and giggled. She and Amber loved being popular. Tormenting a kid like Oliver was just their idea of a good time.

When Oliver puckered up, Ashley dug around in her new pink knapsack. Her manicured fingers closed around an orange. She put it to Oliver's lips. Still in dreamland, he kissed the fruit.

As the kids around him shrieked with laughter, Oliver woke with a start. He saw the orange, smeared with lipstick, and smacked his forehead.

"Oh, man!" he cried. "Not again!"

"Meet your new girlfriend," Amber

taunted. She grabbed the orange from Ashley and waved it in front of his face.

"Hey, Oken," called a popular boy named Donny, "is she your main *squeeze*?" He turned to the crowd of kids around Oliver. "Get it, *squeeze*? *Orange*? Where do I come up with this stuff?"

As Donny high-fived his friends, two girls pushed their way through the gawking group. One of them was Miley Stewart.

Miley was a good friend of Oliver's. She was also Hannah Montana, the hottest teen pop singer around. She lived in a fabulous Malibu beach house. She had millions of fans. And she was very good at keeping her rock star life a secret. Unfortunately, Miley *wasn't* very good at keeping Oliver out of trouble.

"Hey, leave him alone!" Miley yelled.

"Yeah," said her best bud, Lilly Truscott.

Lilly was a tomboy, a skateboarding fanatic, and she wasn't afraid of anyone. In other words, she was great to have around during face-offs like this. She and Oliver were the only friends of Miley who knew about her secret Hannah Montana life.

"Nobody picks on Oliver but *us*," Lilly declared.

"That's right!" Oliver agreed. Then he realized *what* he was agreeing to. "Hey!"

Miley shook her head at the sight of his pink glossed mouth. "I mean, if we were going to pick on Oliver, we easily could've said, 'Man, you make an *ugly* girl.'"

Lilly nodded. "But we didn't . . . even though it's true."

"Thanks!" said Oliver. "Hey!"

Just then, the classroom door opened, and in came the teacher. "Okay, people," said Mr. Picker, clapping his hands. "It's pop quiz time!"

The class moaned as they took their seats. And Mr. Picker smiled. He *loved* the sound of students moaning in the morning!

"Who can tell me why this is the worst day of my life?" he asked.

Like a wild man, Oliver waved his hand.

In the seat behind him, Milo smacked his forehead. "Don't do it," he warned his friend. "You *never* get this right."

But Oliver was in his own little world, totally determined to answer. "I know why it's the worst day of your life, Mr. Picker!" he blurted out. "You got passed over for principal again, right?"

Mr. Picker frowned and narrowed his eyes. "That's right, Oken, poke the bear with a stick, why don't you? *No*, it's not that—" The teacher finally noticed Oliver's lipstick. "And by the way," Mr. Picker told him, "that's not your color."

Oliver blushed pinker than the makeup on his mouth. He wiped it off with his sleeve.

"Anyway," the teacher continued, pulling papers from his briefcase, "my *joy* today is because I lost a bet with Coach Hendricks and am now the chaperone of this year's class camping trip."

Once again, the class moaned.

"Oh, don't moan. It's going to be great," Mr. Picker told them. ". . . Sitting by the campfire, telling stories, being eaten alive by disease-ridden bugs . . ." The teacher sighed and shook his head. "How did Hendricks fit an entire cantaloupe in his mouth? I saw it and I still don't believe it."

"Oh, come *on*," Miley drawled, her Southern accent coming out. "Campin's fun. I do it all the time."

Mr. Picker raised an eyebrow. "Little Miley Sunshine, trying to turn my frown upside down?"

Miley nodded. Then, just for good measure, she threw the man one of her dazzling Hannah Montana grins. Now if *that* don't take the grump out of the guy, she thought, I'll eat my glitter sunglasses.

"That's very sweet," Mr. Picker told her, "and, at this moment, *incredibly annoying!*"

Miley frowned. So much for that, she thought. And I am *not* eating my sunglasses, thank you very much.

"Now get your parents to sign these forms," Mr. Picker told the class as he pulled them out of his briefcase. "So you can spend twenty-four glorious hours with me and *no* indoor plumbing."

"Ewwww!" cried Amber and Ashley.

Miley rolled her eyes. *Princess alert*, she

thought. But then, it figures the prissy twins would be grossed out. They'd probably never even *seen* an outhouse before, let alone used one.

Miley, on the other hand, didn't have any problem with the great outdoors. She loved camping and she'd had plenty of experience with the no-flush throne. In fact, according to her dad, one of their distant relatives still lived—as he put it—the "rustic" life back home in Tennessee. Translation: he had an outhouse.

Of course, the A-for-Attitude girls were far from happy about the idea. As Mr. Picker started passing out the permission forms, they began complaining.

"I don't want to go to the bathroom in the woods," Ashley whined.

"I don't even like going *here*!" Amber cried.

Miley spoke up, hoping she could change their minds.

"Just think about it," she drawled in her country girl voice. "Campin' under the stars, breathin' all that fresh mountain air, surrounded by the sounds o' nature . . ." Miley paused to create some convincing backwoods sound effects—bird whistles, owl hoots, and chipmunk calls.

Amber and Ashley shuddered.

"*What* are you doing?" Amber snapped.

Miley threw up her hands. "A chipmunk, *duh*," she replied.

Amber made a disgusted face. And Ashley lifted her chin. "Could you *be* any more of a hillbilly?" she asked.

Miley shook her head and thought, If that girl's nose gets stuck any higher, she'll be sniffing the ceiling!

"Well, I could've done a pig," she told

them, "but you guys already got that covered."

As Amber and Ashley sputtered, trying
(and failing) to come up with a comeback,
Lilly joined in the fun.

"Mmm, what's that I smell?" she asked
wryly. "Bacon that just got *burned*!"

Ashley narrowed her eyes. "Geeks," she
spat.

"Freaks," Miley countered.

Amber and Ashley pointed their fingers
first at Miley, next at Lilly. "Loser! . . .
Loser! . . . Ooh!" they cried. Then they
touched their fingers together and made a
sizzle sound.

Like they're hot, Miley thought. *Not!*

"Do that stupid finger thing one more
time," threatened Lilly with a raised fist,
"and I will—"

Just then, Miley noticed Mr. Picker

walking toward them with his permission forms.

"Ooh, catfight on aisle five," he declared.

Miley gulped, seeing visions of detention dancing in her head—along with a *canceled* Hannah rehearsal!

"Sir," she quickly jumped in, trying to save the situation, "we were just talking about what a kick it was going to be to get to know each other better." She bobbed her head so hard she felt like a dashboard ornament. "Right, guys?"

Lilly, Amber, and Ashley followed her lead. Now they all looked like bobble-head dolls!

"Oh, yeah!" they cried. "You bet! . . . Uh-huh!"

"Good," said Mr. Picker, "you're sharing the same tent."

"*WHAT?*" the girls cried together.

Miley had seen group hugs. But she'd never before witnessed group *horror* — until now!

"Oh, you don't *want* to share the same tent?" Mr. Picker asked, looking all concerned.

For a second, the girls felt relieved. They were sure the teacher was going to reassign them. But, with a look of twisted glee, Mr. Picker said, "Even better!"

Then he slapped the forms on their desks, turned to Miley, and asked, "How do you like camping *now*, chipmunk?"

Chapter Two

On the day of the camping trip, Miley got up extra early. She heard a familiar deep voice floating up from the first floor.

To anyone else, it would have sounded as if Robby Stewart was working on a new hit tune for Hannah Montana. But Mr. Stewart was more than Miley's songwriter and manager. He was also her father. And Miley had his number. She knew *exactly* what he was doing in their living room.

"Ninety-eight . . . I see ya," Mr. Stewart

sang, ". . . ninety-nine . . . I'm coming to get'cha . . . one hundred. Come 'ere, darlin', time to dance!"

Miley's dad finished his one hundred sit-ups and snatched his reward—the gooey piece of cake on the coffee table.

Still in her pajamas, Miley watched from the top of the stairs. *Perfect*, she thought. Now that Dad's all sugared up, this will be easy!

She uncapped her red marker and drew a few more little red dots on her face and arms. Then she tossed the marker away.

Fake rash in place, she thought. *Check!* And now for the fake coughing spell.

Cough-cough . . . cough-cough . . . cough-cough-cough! She hacked as she moved down the stairs.

Her dad hadn't noticed yet, but Miley kept it up. The trick is in the rhythm, she figured. Just like any good Hannah performance. *Cough-cough . . . cough-cough . . . cough-cough-cough!*

"Hey, buddy," said Mr. Stewart, licking icing off his fingers, "you look terrible."

"Couldn't sleep," said Miley in a fake raspy voice. "Feel sick." And now for the death rattle she'd been practicing for the last half hour.

"Whoa," said her father, hearing Miley's labored breathing. "You sound like that mule who used to carry fat Uncle Earl up the hill to church. . . . And look at that rash! There's no way you're going on that camping trip today."

"But, Daddy," said Miley, pausing to cough some more. "I'm fine."

Miley swayed as if she were really woozy. Then she dramatically fell on the couch. *Wow!* she thought. I deserve an

Oscar for this performance!

Miley's dad looked very concerned. He put a hand on her forehead. "Sorry, darlin'," he said, gravely shaking his head. "You're going back to bed."

As he turned away, Miley bit her lip to keep from singing out, *Vic-to-ry!*

"I'll just have to cancel that interview," said Miley's dad, reaching for the phone. "You know, the one Hannah Montana was going to give Taylor Kingsford?"

"Taylor Kingsford?!" Miley leaped to her feet and yanked the phone out of her father's hand. "He's the coolest VJ on TV! This is awesome!"

Miley's dad raised an eyebrow. The gravely ill girl was *apparently* no longer woozy, raspy, or weak. In fact, she looked fit as a fiddle.

Suddenly, Miley realized what she'd

done. She tried to cough again. But now *she* knew that *he* knew exactly what was going on.

"Nice try," her father quipped. "But next time you might want to go for a *waterproof* rash." He held up the hand that he'd placed on her forehead. There were red stains all over his palm.

Miley gulped. "I'm healed," she tried weakly. "Hallelujah?"

Mr. Stewart folded his arms. "Miley, I know you don't want to share a tent with Amber and Ashley, but sometimes you've just got to make the best of a bad situation."

"Well, in that case," said Miley, "I'm going to need a jar of honey, a thousand red ants, and the cover of nightfall!"

"Times like this, you remind me of your mom," said Mr. Stewart.

Miley's mother had passed away three

years before. And he often told Miley how much she took after her.

"Look, Mile," said Mr. Stewart. "I know those girls don't treat you right, but sinking down to their level isn't the answer."

Miley tapped her chin, thinking it over. "How do we really know that until we *try*?"

Mr. Stewart shook his head. "Remember that kid back home who always teased Jackson, so Jackson snuck into his bathroom to glue his toilet seat?"

Oh, yeah, Miley remembered. Her older brother Jackson had plenty of smarts, but not a lot of common sense. The bullying kid never knew what happened. But Jackson came home with his blond hair soaking wet, a toilet seat glued to his forehead, and a screwdriver glued to his hand.

"It would've worked if I hadn't slipped!" her brother had wailed.

Miley laughed at the memory. "He sure brightened up that crowd in the emergency room!"

"Aw, good times, good times," her father agreed. Then he cleared his throat and refocused. "My *point* is, when you lie down with dogs, you're going to get up with fleas."

"Not if I wear a flea collar!" Miley argued.

Mr. Stewart sighed. He could see he just wasn't getting through to his little girl. So he sat her down and looked straight into her eyes. "Mile," he said firmly, "I'm asking you as a favor to be the *better person* here."

Miley grit her teeth in frustration. "But I already *am* the better person, why do I have to act like it?"

"*Promise* me," her father insisted.

Miley sighed in defeat. She could see her dad was all too serious about this. "Okay, fine," she promised.

Mr. Stewart smiled. "That's my girl!"

DING, DING, DING, DING, DING!

Miley and her father jumped at the sound of the security alarm going off.

Was there a break-in? Miley wondered.

Mr. Stewart raced to the back door. But the door was closed and the lock was set.

"Aw, man!" he cried, realizing what had happened. "That dang mouse is chewing on the wires again!"

Miley watched her dad stomp to the kitchen and grab a skillet. "That's it," he exclaimed, raising the pan. "I'm going to—"

"Oh, no, you're not!" Miley squealed, leaping in front of her dad. "That mouse is a living creature. I've even given it a name . . . *Linda*. It's Spanish for 'pretty.'"

"Well," replied Mr. Stewart, "you better start learning the Spanish for 'squished'!"

Chapter Three

Oliver Oken was ready for the great outdoors. He had his big game hunter's vest. He had his bushman's hat. He had his video camera. And, most important of all, he had his fake Australian accent.

"It was the sixth day without food," he declared. "Only one man could guide the remaining survivors to safety. Oliver Oscar Oken. The Triple O—known the world over as *Ooo*."

Miley rolled her eyes. Oliver had been

recording himself on video since they'd piled onto the school bus. Now that they'd arrived at the campsite, she'd just about had it with the crocodile hunter act.

"Knock it off, Ooo!" she told him.

But Oliver was just getting started. He swung the camera to focus on Miley's face. "It's the Malibu Miley cat!" he cried. "Very rare, very vicious!"

Suddenly, the camera was yanked from Oliver's hands. It was Donny. He turned the camera around to film Oliver.

"And this is the Dorkus Oliverus!" he exclaimed. "Very rare, very stupid."

Donny cackled with his posse of friends. "You hear that? *Dorkus Oliverus*! 'Cause he's a dork." Donny slapped his knee. "I'm on fire!"

Oliver snatched his camera back. But before he could say anything to Donny,

Mr. Picker began to clap his hands.

"Okay, people," the teacher announced, "time for another pop quiz. Could there possibly be a better place to study nature?"

As Oliver began to raise his hand, Milo grimaced. He had seen Oliver fall for the "pop quiz" game too many times to count.

"No!" Milo cried, lunging to pull down Oliver's arm.

Mr. Picker pointed at Milo. "Wrong," he said.

Milo smacked his forehead.

"The answer is *yes*," declared Mr. Picker. "There is a better place to study nature — on a forty-two-inch, high-def, plasma-screen TV in my den — steps away from *indoor* plumbing!" To make his point, the teacher glanced at the campsite's Porta-John and shuddered.

"Come on, Mr. Picker," said Miley,

stepping up. "You can't enjoy the smell and feel of nature on your TV."

"That's the whole point," he replied, slapping a bug off his arm. "Now set up your tents and get into them where I can't see you. And, remember, if you have any questions, pray for a forest ranger 'cause that's what I'll be doing."

Like the other kids, Miley took off her backpack and picked out a spot to set up her tent. The campsite itself was very pretty. Large, old trees and flowering bushes surrounded a clearing of low grass. Miley could hear the birds singing and the familiar burbling of a nearby creek.

Here's a good spot, she thought. Better get to it. She started removing the tent from its canvas bag, when she felt a hard tap on her shoulder. She looked up to find Lilly pointing across the clearing.

"There they are," she whispered.

Amber and Ashley were sitting under a tree, comparing nail polish shades. Miley's tent-mates were obviously blowing off the work of setting up their home away from home.

Lilly pulled a slingshot out of her pocket. "I've got a clear shot," she declared.

"Lilly, wait," Miley said, stepping in front of her, "you could get in trouble. Let me handle this."

Lilly thought it over. "Okay," she finally agreed, "but make it *hurt*."

Miley sighed. "You can count on that," she promised. Then she approached Amber and Ashley, remembering what her father had said. I'm not supposed to sink to their level, she reminded herself.

"Okay," she told the girls, "I know we've had our problems, but Lilly and I are willing to forget all that if you are—"

A hard yank on her arm interrupted her. It was Lilly, pulling her away. "I thought you said it was going to hurt!" she hissed.

"Trust me," said Miley. "It was the most painful thing I've ever done. But I promised my dad I'd be the better person."

"Well, I didn't!" Lilly noted. She lifted her slingshot again.

"Lilly, I can't pull this off without you," begged Miley. "Come on. Help me."

Lilly folded her arms. "Why?"

"Because," said Miley, "you're my friend."

"No," she said.

"Then help me because it's the right thing to do," Miley pleaded.

"*Ohhhh*, no," said Lilly.

"Then help me because . . . I'm on *The Taylor Kingsford Show* tomorrow night," said Miley. "And if you don't, I'm not taking you."

Lilly's eyes widened, and her jaw dropped. Two seconds later, she was swooping down on Amber and Ashley with a huge, fake smile. "Hello, tent pals!" she cheerfully exclaimed. "Who wants me to braid their hair?"

Amber and Ashley grimaced at Lilly's grubby tomboy fingers. "Ewww!" they cried.

Miley stepped up and put on her own fake smile—which, she discovered, was a *whole* lot harder than putting on a fake rash.

"Oh, come on," she said. "Whadya say we put up this tent, make a fire, and cook us up a big pot of friendship?"

Ashley rolled her eyes. "We'd like to," she told Miley, "but we don't speak *Hillbilly.*"

"Or do our wash down yonder in the *crick,*" Amber added.

Miley remembered her promise to her dad. Clenching her fists, she forced herself to laugh. Elbowing Lilly, she got her best friend to join in.

"I hate them," Lilly whispered to Miley through fake chuckles.

"Taylor Kingsford, Taylor Kingsford," Miley quietly reminded her between her own fake ha-has.

Ashley and Amber narrowed their eyes with suspicion on the laughing Miley and Lilly. Then they rudely turned away.

"You know what I'm thinking, Ash?" said Amber.

"Half-caff-" said Ashley.

"-nonfat-" added Amber.

"-grande-latte-with-just-a-sprinkle-winkle-of-cinnamon. Ooh," the girls said together. Then they touched fingers as if they were on fire. "Ssss . . ."

Lilly couldn't take it. As the prissy pair headed toward a forest footpath, she pulled out her slingshot again. "That's it," she told Miley, taking aim. "I'm going to sprinkle their winkles!"

"No! Remember Taylor Kingsford!" cried Miley. She lunged to wreck Lilly's aim just as the girl released her shot.

"Ow!" cried Mr. Picker.

Miley cringed. She'd wrecked Lilly's aim, all right. The slingshot had missed Amber and Ashley—and hit their teacher!

Lucky for them, the man had been bending over at the time.

"That's a bite!" exclaimed the teacher. He'd already been freaking out over the insects. Now he grabbed his stinging rear end and cried, "That's a *big* bite."

Chapter Four

While Miley's teacher thought he was being bitten, Miley's father and brother were trying to *get* a bite. They'd set a trap— complete with some delicious cheese—to catch the mouse. But somehow the mouse had stolen the cheese from right under their noses!

Mr. Stewart clenched his fists. Losing was something he had always taken in stride. But losing to a rodent was *humiliating*!

Meanwhile, back at camp, Miley's best friend was having a meltdown.

"Well, this is just great!" Lilly cried. "Amber and Ashley bail, and now we have to put this thing up all by ourselves!"

Lilly was so angry, she couldn't even look at Miley. She just paced back and forth, staring at the ground. "I mean, ask me to change the trucks on a skateboard. I can do that. But a tent? This'll take forever!"

When Lilly finally looked up, she saw Miley standing next to a fully assembled tent. Lilly's jaw dropped. The thing was so perfectly put together, it could have been a display model at a camping store!

"How did you—" she began.

But Miley waved her hand. "When you're raised in Tennessee, they teach you this before you're potty trained," she said. "Look inside, there's cut flowers."

As Lilly checked out the interior, Miley heard a commotion nearby. Together, she and Lilly followed the noise. They found a tangle of fabric, poles, and ropes on the ground—and two boys arguing in the middle of it.

"Donny," said Oliver, "I don't think it goes that way."

"You should've stopped that sentence after 'I don't think'!" Donny declared. Then he turned to his crew of friends. "Did you hear that? 'I don't think!' 'Cause he *doesn't think*! . . . I own him!"

Donny's followers laughed. And Oliver clenched his fists. "Yeah," he shot back at Donny, "well, *you* should've stopped after . . . uh, 'Did you hear that? Did you hear that?'"

Milo stepped up to Oliver. "They heard

it," he whispered. "That's why they're not laughing."

Oliver frowned. Okay, he thought, so my insult made absolutely no sense. So what! I'm going to put this tent up *my* way!

He grabbed one end of the spring-loaded fabric and pulled it toward him. But Donny wasn't about to let Oliver win. So he grabbed the other end.

"Oh, come on," Donny taunted, "you can pull harder than that, Olivia!"

Oliver narrowed his eyes. "Oh, you're going to regret that, Don . . . na!"

Lilly giggled at that. But Miley wasn't laughing. She could see the boys needed a referee. With the tent frame bowing all the way to the ground, she moved over it and stood right between them.

"Step aside, rookies," she confidently declared. "Let me show you how to do this."

But Oliver didn't step aside. Instead, he pulled his end harder. "I can do it if he'd just let go!"

Donny shook his head. "You let go!"

Just then, both Donny and Oliver lost their grips. The tent flipped upward and Miley was caught in the middle.

"Tent wedgie, tent wedgie!" she cried. The spring-loaded contraption snapped up between her legs and left her hanging upside down.

This is bad, she thought, holding on tight. But it could be worse. And a minute later, it *was*. Amber and Ashley returned from their wilderness walk.

"No place to buy a latte," whined Amber, "no place to buy shoes, and not a single multiplex. Why would anyone want to come to the woods?"

Ashley nodded in agreement. "It's

nothing but trees. What a waste of space!"

Just then, the two girls noticed the tent that Miley had put up. "Are we supposed to sleep in this?" Amber asked. She ran her hand over the fabric. "It's synthetic!"

"Ewwww." The two girls cringed in horror.

Miley rolled her eyes, watching the prissy pair from her upside-down perch. She almost didn't see Mr. Picker walking right up to her.

"What are you doing?" the teacher asked.

Duh, thought Miley. Isn't it obvious? "Pitching a tent," she replied.

Mr. Picker raised an eyebrow. "How's that working out for you?"

Miley shrugged. "I'm hangin' in."

"Great," said the teacher, throwing up

his hands. "I have so many bites on my tush, it looks like a waffle."

"Yoo-hoo, Mr. Picker?" called Amber, waving her hand.

When the teacher looked over, Ashley pointed to the tent Miley had erected and asked, "Did we build *ours* the right way?"

"What?!" cried Miley. She was so shocked by Ashley's lie that she let go of her perch and dropped like a rock.

Dang, that smarts, Miley thought as she scrambled to her feet. But Mr. Picker was already gone. He'd moved next door to check out her tent.

"Wow, I'm impressed," he told Amber and Ashley. "You should see mine. I threw it in the lake."

"But *Miley* put up that tent!" Lilly cried, running over to defend her best friend. "*They* just went for lattes!"

Amber and Ashley threw Lilly a look of total disbelief. "Lattes?" Amber repeated.

"In the forest?!" Ashley cried.

Then Amber shook her head. "I can't believe you would try to take credit for something we did."

"All we wanted to do was put up a tent, make a fire, and cook us up a big pot of friendship," Ashley proclaimed.

"That's what I said!" Miley cried.

But Amber wasn't about to admit it. "She's taking credit again!" she whined. "Mr. Picker, make her stop."

Mr. Picker put a hand to his throbbing head. "If it'll make *you* stop, sure," he told her. "Here's a thought: why don't you just apologize to each other, or at the very least fake an illness so we can all *go home.*"

Miley could see she'd been trumped. Choking back her anger, she spit out, "Fine . . . I'm sorry."

Now it was Lilly's turn to apologize. But, by now, she was so angry she was actually shaking. Miley nudged her. And Lilly finally opened her mouth.

"Right," said Lilly. "We're both sorry . . . that you two are evil, lying loads of *nasty*!"

That evening, Miley and Lilly were not happy campers. Mr. Picker had assigned the two to KP duty. Miley didn't know what those letters meant, but she suspected the *P* stood for pain in the neck!

She and Lilly were stuck cleaning all the plates, cups, and utensils the students used at dinner. I can't believe it, Miley thought, bent over a tub of soapsuds. Every other kid here gets to sit around the campfire, toasting marshmallows. And what do I get? *Dishpan hands!*

"A little tip," Mr. Picker told Lilly as he handed her his empty coffee cup. "In the future, when apologizing, leave out the phrase, 'lying loads of *nasty*.'"

Suppressing a chuckle, the teacher headed back to the campfire. A minute later, Oliver walked over and handed Miley his dinner plate.

"Here," he said.

Miley washed the dish. Then Lilly dried it and placed it on the mile-high stack they'd already cleaned. That's when Miley noticed Oliver hadn't returned to the campfire. He just stood there, looking almost as miserable as she felt.

"What's your problem?" Miley asked.

Oliver sighed. "I have to share a tent with Donny tonight."

"So?" asked Lilly.

"He had *five* helpings of beans!" Oliver exclaimed.

"Oh, come on, Oliver," said Miley, "it's not like he did it on purpose."

"I think he *did*," Oliver replied, pointing at the campfire. Donny was grinning in their direction. With one hand, he pointed at Oliver. With the other, he fanned his rear end.

Defeated, Oliver returned to the campfire. And Amber and Ashley approached Miley and Lilly.

"Look, we feel bad about this," Amber began. "We didn't know he'd make you wash all the dishes."

"But, look, you're *almost* done," said Ashley. Then she dropped her plate into the sudsy tub and accidentally-on-purpose knocked over their tower of clean plates.

"Oops, sorry," Ashley said. "See? I can apologize."

Amber put an arm around her friend's shoulders. "Well, that's because *you're* the bigger person."

As the two toddled away laughing, Miley turned to Lilly. Too outraged to say a word, she grabbed Lilly's hand, slapped it over her own mouth, and screamed into it. Then she calmly removed her friend's hand and said, "Thank you."

"Forget Taylor Kingsford," Lilly told Miley in a calm voice. "I'm going after them, and don't try to stop me."

"Who's stopping you? I'm going with you!" Miley declared. That prissy pair had finally gone too far. "Sorry, Dad," she whispered. "Get the flea dip ready, 'cause tonight I'm lyin' down with the dogs."

Chapter Five

As night fell over the forest, the stars came out. The students went into their tents. And, without a word to each other, Miley, Lilly, Amber, and Ashley climbed into their sleeping bags.

Just as Amber and Ashley dozed off, a loud rustling sound outside awoke Amber. "What was that?" she whispered. Sitting up in alarm, she flipped on her flashlight. "Ashley . . . Ashley!"

Ashley was still dreaming about a typical

day at school. "Move your hand," she mumbled. "I can't see your answers."

As the rustling continued, Amber smacked her girlfriend on the shoulder.

"Ow!" cried Ashley, finally waking up.

Lilly rolled over. "What's going on?" she asked through a yawn.

"I heard something outside," Amber whispered.

Miley waved her hand. "It was probably just the wind"—suddenly, she heard a low, guttural growl—"or not," Miley revised with a gulp. She quickly sat up, and so did Lilly.

By this time, Amber and Ashley were close to terrified. "Mr. Picker!" they called in a strangled whisper. "Mr. Picker!"

Mr. Picker's tent wasn't far, but there was no way he was going to hear Amber and Ashley calling. The man had slapped a sleep mask over his eyes and stuck plugs in his ears.

"Just hold it in, Picker," he chanted to himself, "twelve more hours, you can do it . . ."

Meanwhile, in Miley's tent, things went from bad to worse. The menacing growl had gotten louder and closer.

"What is that thing?!" Amber cried.

"Don't know," said Miley, her eyes widening. "Could be a bear, a mountain lion . . ."

Lilly looked scared, too. "Whatever it is, it sounds hungry."

GRRRRRRRRR! BAM!

Something powerful struck the tent. It swayed back and forth like a carnival ride, and Amber and Ashley totally freaked.

"I'm too pretty to get eaten!" Ashley squealed.

She tried to shove Amber in front of her.

But Amber protested. "Hey," she said, "I'm pretty, too!"

"I'll mention that at your funeral!" Ashley promised, still struggling to throw her best friend to the wolves, the lions, or whatever other wild animals were out there!

Miley couldn't take it anymore. She kicked off her sleeping bag and got to her feet.

"Miley, what are you doing?" Lilly asked.

"If we stay in here, we'll get torn to pieces," Miley replied. "Our only hope is if I can get to the ranger station alive."

Lilly violently shook her head. "Miley, this is stupid. I just can't let you go."

"But, *we* can!" cried Amber.

"Go, go!" Ashley urged Miley. "Be stupid!"

Before Lilly could stop her, Miley was moving to the tent's front flap. "Don't worry," she said, halfway out. "I'm going to be just *f-i-i-i-i-i-i-i-ne*!"

Amber and Ashley screamed as Miley was yanked right out of their midst.

On the other side of the tent, Miley whispered, "Thanks for the help."

Oliver shrugged. "Anything to get out of Donny's tent," he said. "He got a standing ovation from the skunks."

"Ready?" she whispered.

He nodded and lifted the stick in his hand. Then Oliver began to make growling and yelping sounds.

"Oh, no, you don't!" Miley cried.

Oliver beat the tent with his stick.

"Yeah, that's right!" Miley called. "Not so tough now . . ."

A second later, Oliver broke the stick.

"Ow, my leg!" Miley squealed.

Oliver picked up a second stick and broke it.

"And my other leg!" she cried.

Oliver broke a third stick, and Miley glared at him. "And my arm!" she added, but thought, *Enough already!*

Meanwhile, back inside the tent, Amber and Ashley were having a total meltdown. Amber grabbed Lilly by the shoulders. "Okay, you go next," she demanded.

"Why me?" squeaked Lilly.

Ashley rolled her eyes. "I think we've established the 'pretty scale.'"

Lilly glared at them, but they didn't care. When Miley's head appeared through a flap in the back of the tent, they shrunk back in horror.

"Lilly, he's got me!" Miley exclaimed.

"Oh, no, he doesn't!" Lilly cried. She tried to pull Miley back inside. But it was no use.

"It's too late," Miley called. "Good-bye!"

Her head disappeared. And the girls heard her scream, "Ahhhh!"

Lilly freaked. "No, Miley, no!" She pushed her own head through the back flap. "Hey! You let her go, you—*whoa*!"

Lilly was pulled right out of the tent. And Amber and Ashley stared in shock. The growling, snarling animal that had eaten Miley had just gotten Lilly, too!

Outside, hiding in the bushes, Miley, Lilly, and Oliver bit their tongues to keep from laughing. Then they stepped out of the bushes, found some tree branches, and began to beat the tent nonstop.

Amber and Ashley came flying out of their synthetic fortress, screaming like crazed Hannah Montana fans. But there was no encore needed at this performance.

They raced straight to the Porta-John,

fighting with each other to get inside. But when they pulled open the door, they found Donny inside. The baron of beans was washing his hands.

"Hey! *Occupado*!" Donny protested.

Amber and Ashley didn't care. They forced their way inside and closed the door.

"Get out!" Donny demanded.

"You get out!" Ashley shrieked.

The Porta-John began to rock violently back and forth until it finally fell over. "Ahhhhhh!" they all screamed. Then came a great big, grossed-out "Ewwwwwww!"

Miley, Lilly, and Oliver celebrated with high fives. Lilly grinned as she pulled out her camera phone and took aim.

"Looks like my daddy was wrong," said Miley, posing in front of the outhouse. "I got down with the dogs, and got up *flea free*."

Chapter Six

The next afternoon, VJ Taylor Kingsford was just about ready to interview Hannah Montana.

"And that was Hannah Montana's latest pop music video!" he announced to the television camera. "Stick around, in a minute we'll be back with the real deal. I love you! I mean it!"

A second later, the stage manger called, "And we're clear!"

With his show in a commercial break,

Taylor walked over to Hannah. She was waiting in the wings.

"There you are," he called, "looking fine!"

Dressed in her long, blond Hannah wig, cool sunglasses, and glittery clothes, Miley smiled big.

"And who's your wing-woman?" Taylor asked.

Standing right beside Hannah was Lilly, although no one would be able to tell; she was dressed in her Lola Luftnagle disguise.

Lilly stared wide-eyed at Taylor for a minute. Then she began to giggle hysterically.

Taylor leaned toward Hannah. "Is she all right?" he whispered.

Hannah shook her head. "I ask myself that question every day." Just then, her cell phone rang. She answered the call. It was Oliver.

"What do you want?" she asked impatiently. "I'm almost on."

Oliver was calling from his bathroom, where he'd been slathering his legs and arms with calamine lotion.

"Listen, Miley, this is important!" he told her. "Remember that bush we were standing in outside your tent? It was poison oak!"

"That's crazy. If it was, I'd be"—Miley froze—"doing *this*!"

And what was "this"? *Scratching!* Miley suddenly realized she'd been scratching her arms for the last few minutes.

"Baby girl," called Taylor from the TV set, "if you want to be on the *show*, you need to be on the *stage*."

"Got to go," Miley told Oliver. She snapped her phone closed and crossed the stage to her seat.

"Okay," she whispered to herself, waiting for the stage manager's signal, "this scratching is just in my head. It's just because he said it. I mean, Lilly isn't—"

She glanced offstage and saw Lilly desperately trying to scratch her own back. The girl was rubbing against a piece of the stage set like a bear against a tree!

Uh-oh, thought Miley, feeling the exact same itch begin to tickle her, too. This is *so* not good.

"We're back," the stage manager warned, "in three, two . . ."

"And we're back with Hannah Montana," said Taylor Kingsford. "Hannah, welcome. I'm just itching to ask you a few questions."

"And I'm *itching* to answer them," she said, squirming in her seat. If only you could do us both a favor, she thought, and *scratch* it for me!

"You always come across as so . . .

squeaky clean," said Taylor. "Now let's be real, is that the true Hannah Montana?"

Hannah swallowed hard. The itching was spreading all over—her arms, her legs, her face. But the absolute worst was her back!

"Well," she said, struggling to concentrate on answering Taylor's question, "I've always believed that at the end of the day it's about loving others"—she spread her arms out wide—"as you would love yourself."

"Boring!" Taylor replied as Hannah quickly brought her arms back in to scratch them.

"Come on," he challenged, "haven't you ever sunk down and done something . . . b-a-a-a-d?"

"Yes," she confessed, rubbing her itchy back against the back of her chair. "And I learned . . . *just recently* . . . that when you lie down with dogs you *do* get up with fleas!"

"Are you okay?" asked Taylor, seeing his guest begin to claw her neck like a flea-bitten puppy.

"Never better!" Hannah lied. "I've just been, uh . . . working on a new dance routine . . ." She scratched some more. "And I can't wait to show you."

Taylor grinned big and faced the camera. "How about that? A Taylor Kingsford sneaky peek!"

"First I need a beat. Give me that mike!" Hannah demanded.

She put the microphone to her mouth, as if she were about to start singing. But the itch became so bad she started using it as a back scratcher.

ZIP-ZIP! . . . ZIP-ZIP-ZIP! . . . ZIP-ZIP!

"Oh, yeah, oh, yeah," said Hannah in relief.

But to Taylor, it sounded like a hip-hop beat. "Come on, band," he called, bobbing his head to her back-scratching rhythms, "help her out!"

ZIP-ZIP! . . . ZIP-ZIP-ZIP! . . . ZIP-ZIP!

"Contagious, isn't it?" said Hannah. "Everybody's doing it! See?"

Hannah ran offstage and dragged Lilly back on to help her out. "I call it the scratch dance!" Hannah cried. She handed Lilly the mike. "A little to the left," she instructed her, "now a little to the right, higher, lower, that's just right! Oh, yeah, oh, yeah, scratch dancin'! Don't stop now! Scratch dancin'!"

"Now switch!" Lilly cried, desperate to get her own itch taken care of.

"You wish!" said Hannah. "Scratch dancin'! Scratch dancin'!"

That night, Miley sat in front of her television, covered in calamine lotion — and shame. "I can't watch this," she told her dad, hiding her eyes.

Her appearance on Taylor Kingsford's show had been taped earlier. Now it was being replayed for the whole country, including her father and brother. And both of them thought the scratch dance was a riot.

"You don't have to watch it," Miley's father told her with a chuckle. "I'm *recording* it. I never get tired of watching me being right."

Jackson jumped up and imitated her dance with silly, exaggerated moves. "Scratch dancin'! Scratch dancin'!" he squealed. "It *is* contagious!"

"If you don't stop it, you're going to find

out!" Miley warned her brother.

Jackson refused to stop, so Miley took off after him. Spreading her rash-covered arms wide, she was just *itching* to give him a nice, big hug!

You better run, Jackson, she thought, because even if my dance isn't contagious, I'm pretty sure my poison oak is!

Put your hands together for the next "Hannah Montana" book. . . .

Super Sneak

Adapted by Laurie McElroy

Based on the series created by Michael Poryes and Rich Correll & Barry O'Brien

Based on the episode, "She's a Super Sneak," Written by Kim Friese

Miley Stewart ran down the stairs and into the kitchen, too excited to notice that her father was cleaning a huge fish. Her brother, Jackson, looked on, trying not to notice that his dinner had eyes.

"Dad, I know I have midterms Monday, but the new Ashton Kutcher movie is previewing tonight!" Miley put her hand on his arm and gazed at him with her absolutely sweetest smile. "How many 'prettys' do I need to put before 'please' for you to let me go?" she asked.

"Now, Mile—" Mr. Stewart said, heading for the refrigerator.

That sounded like the beginning of a no. Miley cut him off. She ducked under his arm and stood between him and the lemons. "Pretty, pretty, pretty, pretty, pretty, pretty please, Dad, please?"

"Whoa!" Mr. Stewart held up his hands in what looked like surrender.

"I can go?" Miley asked excitedly.

"No, you can stop," Mr. Stewart said. "You know you've got to study."

Miley wasn't about to give up. It was Ashton Kutcher, after all. "Yes, Dad, but if you think about it, midterms are halfway to finals, so I only need to study about half as hard," she argued. "And since I already study twice as hard as everybody else, I only need to study a quarter. So I'm done." Miley looked up at her father with a beaming smile. "See how that works?"

It was all perfectly logical to Miley, but her father didn't understand. "No. And you know what? I'm the dad and you lose. See how *that* works?" he asked, calmly picking up a knife and slicing a lemon.

Miley's shoulders slumped. Her two best friends, Lilly and Oliver, were going to the movie preview. So was everybody else. Everybody except Miley. She had to think of a way to get her dad to say yes.

Jackson saw a perfect opportunity to win some points with their dad. "You see, little sister, Dad, as a single parent, is only trying to make sure that you have the proper guidance. And I, for one, commend him on his commitment to education." He walked over and patted Mr. Stewart on the back with a big, fake smile.

Mr. Stewart didn't buy that, either. "Son, I'm glad you feel that way. Because I'm committing you to staying home and studying this weekend, too." He patted Jackson on the back and gave him an equally fake smile.

Jackson's couldn't believe it. His plan totally backfired.